Pure in Heart

By

Troy Anston

ISBN: 1-4140-2145-3 (e-book)
ISBN: 1-4140-2146-1 (Paperback)
ISBN: 1-4140-2147-X (Dust Jacket)

This book is printed on acid-free paper.

1stBooks – rev. 12/03/03

"Blessed are the pure in heart, for they shall see God"

Matthew 5:8

Tables of Contents

Just a Story...

My story is unique. My name, or what I was once known by, was Troy Anston. I'm not called that name anymore. I was once, but that seems like centuries ago. But you, you can call me Trans. That was my nickname. It sort of caught on and eventually even my family got around to calling me by that name. So Trans it is. If you're reading these words than you somehow found this story after I have left. Maybe it even got published somehow and was stuck in some fiction section somewhere, which would be sad really because the story that follows is nothing but a harsh reality. It is the truth that I have decided to put down on paper. The time for action has ended and the time for words is upon us. Please, take what is written and believe it, or you can decide to dismiss it as another weird fantasy story. Either way, it doesn't really matter to me. Just because you might not believe in something, doesn't mean it's not really there.

My life started out like most every other person's life. I was born into a family as the eldest son with a younger sister. The place of my birth is not really important. The story doesn't really hinge on the area I grew up in or on the places I visited during my life. The meaning contained in these words carries within it something deeper; something more profound, and hopefully you will see that truth. But for now, I just wanted you to know that I had a family once and that I tried to grow up like any other normal kid would. But right from the start something was different in me. Nothing too special at first, you understand. I just seemed to learn faster than the other children. OK, you may say, still pretty normal. In fact my parents just believed me bright for my age, as did the other people around me and in my life. Soon after that I matured just like any other kid. It wasn't until I hit those dreaded teenage years that the "special" changes really began to take place. Not the normal ones mind you. Yes, those did occur too. But other things started to happen as well. It was around the age of thirteen that I for the first time realized I had a photographic memory. It suddenly dawned on me that I hadn't forgotten anything I had ever read or seen. It wasn't till I was yet a little older that I learned that my memory wasn't just good, it was perfect. I could walk through a room or look around a corner for a split second and have seen everything there was to see. I could picture in my mind where everything was, what everyone looked like, what they were wearing, what they were drinking, what color eyes they had, everything. I could read a book as fast as I could flip through the pages and I would never forget any of it. Yet, this was not the only change that I would come to understand.

During puberty other things started to happen as well. During normal fitness exercises at school I began to stand out from the others. For an example, when we as a class had to the run the mile for time, I beat everyone else. OK, not too special. There are a lot of fast kids out there. But this was something different. I didn't seem to get tired. I didn't realize this at first; I just thought I was in good shape. But then I started to see things differently. The other kids were panting; obviously tired after the physical exertion they just put themselves

2

through. But I, I felt better, more energized than when I started. I felt I could run longer and even faster after the race was over. In fact, that was just what would happen. As I ran for longer periods of time, I didn't get slower, I got faster and I wouldn't even break a sweat.

Well you can imagine what high school was sort of like for me. I got straight A's in all my classes. Without even trying I could recall the pages of the textbooks where the answers were to be found and after changing the wording in my mind I would write them down. Math seemed to come to me like a second language. I could compute numbers in my head faster and more efficiently than most calculators. My math tests were just a column of answers down the left hand side. I was never very big physically, which gave the other kids an open door to begin making fun of me. In addition I was good in school, which is never a positive thing for a kid who was desperately trying to be cool. So my existence for nearly all of my school-going life consisted of ridicule and name-calling. I was an outcast from the start. Oh, I tried to make friends. Some kids actually let me hang out with them for a while. But in the end it was always the same. My nature, my abilities, whatever it was: It always built up barriers between me and the other kids, and I always ended up alone with no real friends and no one to hang out with.

I never had anyone that I could call a true friend. I did occasionally try and hang out with some kids, but they tended to make fun of me more than not and eventually I just stopped letting them hurt me like that. Life for me, as I was growing up, was hard. The more I tried to fit in the more I seemed to be pushed away. All the

3

while I was ridiculed and teased by those seemingly perfect popular kids who never would let it go. I just wanted so desperately to fit in, yet no matter how hard I tried, nothing seemed to work. Through all of this insecurity, sadness, frustration, and at points, despair, I still never knew the truth about myself. I never knew what was in store for my life and I could have never imagined it if I tried.

Insights into my destiny, if it could be called that, always seemed to come from out of the blue. I discovered one insight into myself by mistake, as was sometimes the usual, and it came at me like a missile and hit me with just as much force. One day, I found myself playing a game of tag after school. Somehow I managed to follow along with a group of guys that I so badly wanted to be accepted by. I was a lanky junior in high school at the time and unbeknownst to me, destined for great things I could never foresee. But back to the issue at hand, this game of tag was different than those I was usually accustomed to when I was younger. The group I was hanging around with was not kids anymore and now a once simple game of tag has become a serious game of competition and an underlying athletic superiority contest. It was a game of stealth, quickness, and cleverness. I was unusually pretty good, because if a person who was "it" didn't get me through stealth and started to give chase, I could outrun them. Well like I said, one day the game was on. I was walking by a row of bushes on a concrete path by some houses in a greenbelt. I was moving with a slow gait, a straight back, not bothering to hide, trying to show these cool guys how confident and cocky I could be. I hoped that I might be considered cooler if I acted like that. All of a sudden, the most popular jock, some football player, jumped for me from the bushes on my left. He nearly had me, but he had moved a bit too early. He reached out, but I had already turned and sprinted off in the opposite direction. This guy thought he had me so he didn't give up there and gave chase. He was quicker than me, but all I needed was a few more steps before my ability kicked in and I was off. Unfortunately it started to look like I wasn't going to get those steps after all, so I did what any other insecure kid trying to impress the cooler kids while playing tag would do. I jumped the row of hedges on my left in a last ditch effort to dodge the tagger. Now here is where that missile I spoke of comes into play. Have you ever jumped something, maybe a flight of stairs, maybe an unknown ledge, without ever knowing exactly how far it was down to the earth on the other side? And just as you cleared the object and your eyes glanced down you realized that the ground was farther than you thought, and you knew you were about to fall, and you knew you were about to get hurt. Well that was what happened to me. I jumped the hedge and realized as I looked down that the ground was a good twenty feet below me and that the ground was made of cement. My stomach dropped. I think I cussed and messed my pants at the same time, and then I fell. Now if there had been water below me, twenty feet is not that far. But when the surface one is racing toward in the air is cement, things are a little different. But, it was not till my feet hit the concrete that the missile I was talking about exploded in my face. I fell faster and faster and then my feet hit the ground. My knees bent to cushion the landing as my body continued downward, and then, that was it. I had hit the ground. But not with the bone crushing force I expected. I landed lightly, almost delicately. Yeah, I did come down fast and no, I didn't slow down in the air and yet somehow I landed as if I just stepped down the final step of a staircase. And all the force and the pain I thought I would feel as my body slammed into the ground became something else I never expected. Instead of expelling the driving force I thought I would exert as I careened down toward the cement, the force seemed to come up from the ground into me. I felt pressure as I landed, but no pain, and the force I expected to eject as I collided actually seemed to flow into me instead. It appeared that the energy I was going to produce and disperse into the earth by slamming into it, in fact moved into my body, filling me from my feet to my head.

I looked up to see the startled faces of those kids that had gathered above me and been relayed the story while I stood shocked below them. They soon raced down to see if I was OK, still unsure of the state I was in. They found out I was fine and were as shocked as I was.

That was the first moment in my life where everything began to change. When I felt that energy enter into me something in my mind clicked. My understanding shifted and I began to see what I was blinded to before. But I couldn't yet be sure. I told the guys that I had to go home, made some lame excuse, and took off running. I don't remember if they called after me, and I don't particularly mind not having heard the words they called after me as I ran. My mind was racing in a thousand directions at once and I couldn't even hear myself think. But one thing was clear now, the effects staring me right in the face. With every step I took, every time my foot came down and struck the ground, I could feel energy flowing into me. Not as much as when I hit the ground after my fall, but each time I brought my feet down to push off again I could feel the faint flow of energy coursing up into me as my feet seemingly bounded off the cement. I could feel myself growing stronger, faster, and more energized with each step I took as I ran off toward home.

It was getting late, but not so much so where I would be expected home any time soon. So I took a detour and ran off toward a construction site for some time alone. The site was empty, as all the workmen had gone home to their families and houses. I wanted to be alone. I wanted to collect my thoughts, and I wanted to see what else I could do. As I gathered myself there at the site, I started to climb the newly constructed frame of a pretty big, soon-to-be apartment complex. It was roughly six stories high. I don't know what possessed me to climb up, but as I climbed up the interior, looking out through the empty spaces where the new walls would soon be, I started to feel a tinge of nervousness rise up in my stomach. I began to think that maybe I was wrong about myself, that maybe I had just landed luckily. Maybe my adrenaline had saved me from hurting myself. I mean, come on, accidentally jumping over a hedge and falling twenty feet was something, but jumping from a building at a construction site was just plain stupid. Doubt poured into my mind and every fiber of my intelligence began to fight against this decision. But still, something deeper inside me helped me press on as I climbed the stairs. Eventually I stood, looking out into the newly fallen twilight, staring six stories straight down to a bunch of compacted and trodden dirt below. Now I was no longer nervous, I was terrified. My mind screamed out against my stupidity and at that same time, something deeper spurred my curiosity and shouted it down. As I looked off into the air feeling stressed and worried, a sudden calm came over me and I just knew I was going to jump. At that moment I felt my body relax, my mind quieted, I took a deep breath, and I jumped soundlessly out into the night, plunging sixty feet down. After a quiet moment and the initial feeling of weightlessness, my eyes sprung open wide in anticipation and fear, riveted on the oncoming, rushing ground. My muscles tightened for the impact I was sure was coming and then I hit the ground.

Everything slowed down at that point. My mind seemed to put everything into slow motion in order for me to be able to take everything in. I felt my body hit the ground with tremendous pressure. But I alighted on my feet, softly again just as before. Almost the exact same instant my feet hit the ground, I felt it happen. Energy rushed into my body. It felt like a dam had been destroyed and the energy from my landing poured forth into my body. So much so, that my eyes flung wide with exhilaration. I had never felt so much energy in all of my life. It flooded into me from the ground, pure and hungry; it rushed eagerly through my body, filling me, consuming me. My mind raced with this newfound power. I looked down at my body and my legs, all seemingly pulsing with strength, I crouched and without thinking, I jumped.

I don't know what I expected to happen. I was acting without thinking now. I felt invincible. I saw myself push off the ground, felt the wind rush through me as I exploded skyward, reveling in the energy and power I felt coursing through me. Then I saw the rooftop of the under-construction apartment building rush past me; that same place where moments before I had leapt out into my destiny. I flew upward past it faster than I fell from it. I looked down as fear gripped my heart and I continued to soar skyward, horrified at what was happening. I panicked as I neared the top of my massive bound. I began to slowly stop in my flight upward; the apartment was a small square, seemingly miles below me. Then I started to fall back to the earth I had apparently tried to escape. I felt gravity regain its control over me as I fell, the wind whipping through my hair and face. Fear froze my heart as panic consumed my mind. I had never fallen before with such force and such speed. I screamed and blacked out. And there I was, hurtling toward the earth, a limp, seemingly lifeless corpse.

In the shadows of a nearby building, three gigantic men stood covered by darkness, their outlines barely visible to prying eyes. Two of the men stood a few feet back from the apparent leader. One of them spoke out in a deep and powerful voice.

"Sir, this is the one? Doesn't look like much."

The giant captain answered, "They never do at first. But we shall see what this one is capable of. I will test him myself."

The giant men stood with watching eyes as the boy lay unconscious in the dirt several yards in front of them. They stood and watched as another man came and found the body and called the police. Then after the boy was taken away, the three men finally turned to go and in an instant, disappeared into the night.

I don't remember much after that, my perfect memory only coming back to me in glimpses of the past. I remember lights, being lifted, and then sleep. The next thing I knew I was in the hospital. It was morning and my parents were standing over me, fear, confusion, anger, and sadness etched on their faces. I awoke to a series of questions, accusations, and worries that only a set of loving parents would subject their child to. From what I gathered from them, they freaked out when I didn't come home, called several people, realized that I was indeed missing and then called the police. Somehow a rent-a-cop security officer doing rounds through the construction site found me, radioed for help, and then the paramedics arrived. One interesting detail I found out later was the story told from the security cop. He said that when he saw me, he naturally came over to see if I was all right. He later said that when he reached out to touch me he was thrown back by an unbelievable force he couldn't explain.

Anyway, the police were baffled as were the doctors. I had obviously passed out, but had no injuries. My parents suspected that I was mugged, but I still had my wallet, and again, no injuries. In fact, I was the perfect example of health. So the only story I could come up with was I was running for a little bit to relieve some stress and must have blacked out from the strain. I told them I was pushing myself pretty hard. They didn't believe a word I said, I'm sure of it, but since they had nothing else to even remotely go with, they took my excuse with a grain of salt and we left the hospital soon after that.

From that experience onward I was scared. I tried to go back to my life as it was before but something in me had changed. I had changed. I kept doing everything the same way I always did before. I aced some tests, avoided the kids that made fun of me at school, and hung out with my family. Life started to return to normal. I refused to test my limits with my ability. I let it sit inside me and tried to be just another normal teenager. This phase lasted for a little while but then again something else inside me shifted and another change occurred.

The Beginnings

It happened suddenly as they always did. I was sitting in class trying not to fall asleep when out of the blue I felt the need to move. No. It was not just a need. It was a command. I had to leave, right now. I had to get outside immediately. I don't know why, I just did. So I raised my hand and pretended I had to go to the bathroom. The teacher waved me off and out I ran from the room. I was in a state of strange panic now and started to run out of the building. Once outside I felt the same command telling me to move, to go somewhere. I can't relay the feeling adequately enough. It just felt like an immediate sense of urgency to go somewhere off to my left. It felt like I had forgotten to do something vital and extremely important and that I had to make up for it now. But the feeling wanted me to go far. It felt like I had to travel an immense distance and I needed to go fast. It was all happening so rapidly that I quickly got confused. I sat down and racked my brain. I still felt the need to move, but not understanding enough to do anything but sit and stare. Then the feeling was gone. The sensation left as quickly as it came. I sat up shocked. I felt no more urge. I felt nothing. And then, I felt worse than nothing. I felt something else crawl into me. It was failure. I felt worthless. I felt like I had done something so wrong that I could never be forgiven. The feeling came at me so fast and so harsh that I nearly started to cry. I couldn't seem to get a grip either. Immense sadness and desperation filled my heart and I sat with tear filled eyes and felt nothing but hurt, sadness, and pain. After countless minutes the feeling slowly began to pass and I drew myself to my feet. Now I did walk to the bathroom and began to wash my face, trying to hide the tears that had sought to escape my eyes. I felt confused and weakened by what had just happened. I had no idea what I just went through; let alone why it happened to me at all. I finally looked into my face in the mirror, tried to shrug off what remained of those feelings, and walked back to class.

I finished off the day, got my stuff together and immediately headed for home. I just wanted to get away from school and leave behind me whatever happened that day. I headed for my house without saying good-bye to anyone, in fact, I was still so shaken that I started to run a little. I felt better almost immediately and by the time I was home, the pain and sadness I felt that day was like a distant memory of a forgotten pain. I greeted my parents and headed upstairs. I wanted to be alone, so I locked myself in my room and stayed there; delving into my thoughts until I fell asleep and my alarm woke me up.

I jumped into the shower and let the water brush the sleep from my eyes. I got dressed and stumbled down the stairs for a quick breakfast. I found my parents and my sister sitting there, just like always. Mom fussing about, sister complaining, trying to get out of going to school, and dad reading the morning paper. I sat down at my seat and started to munch on some toast my mom set down before me as she whisked around the kitchen. I sat contentedly nibbling on my toast when I looked up at my dad and at the paper he held up blocking his face. There on the front page was a picture of a man. My heart froze in my chest. All the feelings I felt the day before ripped into my chest and my mind. Bits of toast fell from my mouth as I gawked noiselessly at the unknown stranger on the front page. I don't know why I did what I did next. It just happened. I grabbed the paper from my father. Said something about forgetting my homework and ran out the front door, grabbing my backpack on the way, and leaving a trail of papers behind me.

I ran for a good ten minutes before stopping in some alley on the way to school. I brought the paper up in front of me and started to speed read down the front page. The man was a local hero. OK, I thought, some cop who saved a bunch of people's lives one day, great. That didn't explain my reaction to his face. That didn't explain why I needed to grab the paper from my dad and run from the house like a psycho. I kept reading and discovered he went missing and presumed dead. Yesterday during work on his drive to some site, he seemed to have pulled his car onto the side of the road. He apparently got out; left the door opened, and disappeared. The sight, according to other officers, had evidence of a struggle, a fight, but that was all. I sat shocked. Desperately trying to find the connection between this lost man and my feelings. Near the end of the page there was a slice from the police report, recording the estimated time of his disappearance. It was the exact time I first felt the pull back at school. My mind was still racing. So what? I thought. Big deal that this man disappeared, I mean, I feel bad, he had a family and stuff, but what did that have to do with me. I sat confused for several moments longer, lost in thought. Finally I looked down at my watch, saw that I was late for school and took off running for class.

Classes that day went by like lightning. I sat through each one, staring ahead, still lost in thought and desperate for answers. Why? Why was this happening to me? What did I do to deserve this stuff? As I continued to ask myself these unanswerable questions I didn't know I would find the answers out soon enough.

First Blood

After school that day I started my walk home. The people I occasionally hung out with all left for various activities and I didn't really feel like trying to join in so I walked off by myself. All this confused the kids at school even more, but it was still too early in my sudden strangeness and I was already tagged as "weird," so my actions hadn't caused too much upheaval yet. As I was walking and thinking of this and other things "it" happened again. That sudden feeling of urgency and the need to move flooded into my mind, pushing everything else out. This time though, the feeling wanted me to move somewhere close. I started to look around, to orient myself. I hadn't been paying to much attention to where I was walking. "There," I thought, "over the houses." My feeling told me to go to the other greenbelt that ran parallel to where I was walking and it told me to go now. This time I acted on instinct. I bolted for the row of houses on my right. I jumped and pulled myself over the nearest gate, landing softly and continued to sprint. I felt some energy begin to enter into me. I kept sprinting around the house and through the side yard. I got to the front and peered out into the greenbelt. As I looked, something inside me told me to get down behind the plants. So I did, but nothing was there in front of me. The feeling still had me in its hold though. It felt like someone was screaming in my mind, urging me to hurry, to do something. "What?" I silently screamed back at the unrelenting desire. There is nothing…. wait! There's a young girl walking toward me. She's coming up the greenbelt. I recognized her. She was a freshman from my high school. Then something else caught my eye. It was a movement in the bushes nearly opposite me. What was it? A dog of some kind my mind told me, but no. It was bigger. It must be a man I thought, but as I watched it move behind the bushes, it didn't move like a man at all. Suddenly, the thing crept out in front of its hiding place. What I saw terrified me beyond anything I have ever felt before.

It looked at first to be a man. Then it took on more of the appearance of a small gorilla. Its arms were clearly too long for its body and it moved with some kind of strange stooped walk, sure enough, using its arms to walk as it moved. The thing was pitch black. Its skin looked hard and leathery. It had a few bristling hairs coming out of its back and chest. And a few other places as well, but they were just as black as the creature itself. To me, it looked like one of my nightmares had just woken up and was out for an afternoon stroll. It looked immensely strong with giant arms and legs, the skin pulled tight across its massive form. It was shorter than me, but much more massive and it walked in an awkward, hunched fashion. Its face was terrible. It had teeth that I could see from where I stood. The things mouth didn't seem to be able to cover all of them and most stuck out of it altogether. The eyes of this thing were a bright yellow and almost appeared to be shining in the midday sun. But the rest of the face looked distorted. This thing was ugly beyond relief and it was then I realized what this thing was. It was an image straight out of my

17

nightmares, a beast of mythic existence that has awoken and walked into my world. This thing was nothing less than a demon., and this demon was doing nothing less than moving straight toward that freshman girl.

I was frozen. It felt like I was watching a horror movie in slow motion. The demon with its slow, hunched over gait, slowly dragging itself toward that young girl, while the girl, seemed to walk, almost skip, happily along, oblivious to the death that slowly approached her. Soon it became obvious to me that she didn't see the creature. I watched in stunned silence. But as the demon staggered closer, something inside me snapped and I woke up. With one confident and powerful move I nearly leapt from my hiding place out into the open. I yelled at the girl to stop moving, which she did in stunned response. Then I turned my eyes on the demon. It quickly took a small leap back, in a move that seemed way too fast and graceful for a thing that was clearly hobbling along a bit earlier. Our eyes met for the first time and I saw things I will never forget flash back at me in those eyes. The demon looked at me with a strange and startled expression. It slowly moved to the left a few steps and then back to the right, starring only at me. I slowly stepped toward the brute. I felt confidence flow into me. I was going to protect this girl. The creature seemed taken aback by my bold gesture. Then something in the demon's eyes shifted. It realized I could see it and hate burned back at me out from under that deformed and hideous visage. I slowly walked forward and put myself between the girl and the beast, never taking my eyes off the creature. In hindsight I don't know why I did this. It seemed like lunacy after the event. But during it all, something inside me took over. Something that would not let this hideous creature hurt that girl. I quickly looked back at her and told her to run back to school. She stayed and stared at me a moment longer, oblivious to the danger of the demon, clueless to what I was actually doing. I told her to run again, this time with anger and strength behind my voice. I wanted her out of here and I wanted her gone now. She gave a small shriek and started to run back the way she came. Then I turned to face the devil.

It came at me slowly, strafing to the right and to the left as it approached. It didn't stagger anymore. It now moved on all fours like a powerful cat. Its hate filled eyes never leaving my own. I watched its muscles tightening under its leathery skin. It moved cautiously and with extreme purpose. It stalked toward me. I held my ground. Trying to stand tall and fearless as the demon moved toward me. Then it happened. With quickness I could barely follow the beast was airborne and with a high, almost ear-shattering scream, came at me with fists raised and mouth, with all its horrible fangs, wide open. I jumped back just in time to escape those two powerful arms as they crashed into the earth in an attempt to drive my head downward into my spine. The ground seemed to tremble with the force of that blow as the demons fists cracked and destroyed the cement walkway. Now I was stunned. The reality of what I was doing quickly dawned on me. I had challenged a demon, one whose strength could crack and shatter cement with a single blow. I had drawn its concentration to me and now I had its full attention. But what concept really started the rise of panic into my head was the speed with which the beast moved. It had jumped and attacked with a quickness I could have never imagined for a beast of its size. Let alone any beast of any kind for that matter. And as I landed from my short leap backward, one massive forearm that had so powerfully crushed the ground a moment before was flung back upwards, connecting on my chest, and knocking me up and away from the ground. After that, I was soaring through the air like a rag doll.

Like I have said a few times before, certain changes have occurred in my life. And if you've paid attention, you'll have noticed that most of them occurred without me knowing when or how. There I am, confused, not able to put the pieces together and see the whole picture and then…. Snap! I see the truth. All of a sudden something is made clear and I finally see what I couldn't before. As I crashed back to earth after that first massive blow, that would have normally collapsed the rib cage of anyone else, I had another realization. That blow that should have killed me actually did quite the opposite, and that same feeling, the one I felt when I accidentally jumped over that hedge and hit the ground, occurred again. As I sailed through the air, a good ten feet up into it to be precise, I felt that familiar energy enter into me. But it did not come from my feet this time. This time it came into me from my chest, from the exact spot my friend "Snuggles the Demon" had just hit me. I felt that energy once again pour through me. I felt it strengthen and empower my whole being, and as I hit the ground and slide in the grass, I felt it increase even more. I was still lying on the ground, enraptured by this new insight, when a shadow fell over my face. I looked up and the shadow seemed to grow larger. It took me a moment to realize that the shadow was growing because the thing that threw me to the ground had jumped and was swiftly coming down from the air in a final attempt to crush the life out of me. I tried to squirm away backward, but I took too long trying to figure out what was happening. The beast was already too close and before I could think I felt two clawed feet land with a tremendous force on my chest. I felt the power course down into me as the creature attempted to crush me into the ground. The pressure was unbelievable as I felt him land and try to smash the life out of me. The beast looked down into my face and a sick smile seemed to be creeping out of its gnarled and distorted mouth. But then, its smile quickly changed. For my eyes were looking back into its and my eyes showed a smile of their own. The beast quickly sprang back off my chest and landed nearly ten feet away. Even as it pushed off I felt more energy flow into my body. I stood up, quickly and powerfully, purpose in my eyes and strength flowing in my blood. The creature shrieked a loud wail of frustration and charged at me again, this time in an attempt to rip my head from my shoulders. It flew straight toward me in a tireless rage, its giant, powerful fist raised to swing. It got within striking range and threw forth a sweeping blow that would have knocked any head clean off. I wasn't about to take a hit again. I raised my left arm quicker than the beast thought I could and quicker than I had ever moved in my whole life. I caught its wrist and easily stopped his blow. A look of shock registered on both of our faces, but my mind moved faster. Before the demon could react, I raised my other arm up above my head and with

21

quickness and speed far faster than the agile demon; I brought it down powerfully on the shoulder of the arm I held. I didn't let go of the beast's arm as I connected with its shoulder. I felt the energy course through me again through my chest and out into my arm. Then I felt something I have never felt before in my life. I felt my arm crack and shatter the shoulder and collarbone of the shrieking and now terrified beast. I let go of the demon's now useless arm. The demon jumped back again in retreat and I watched as the now destroyed arm swung uselessly at the creature's side as it flew backward in the air. But, my mind was not satisfied yet. The demon was not gone, and even with one arm it could still hurt other people. So as the demon sailed back in its jump away from me, I ran forward. I was at the feet of the demon before it even hit the ground. I had never moved so fast in my life. But now, with so much power ebbing through me; a little extra speed didn't seem that strange at all. The demon landed from its jump of retreat and just as its feet landed I was right there in front of it. I reached out and grabbed it by its throat. In two swift and terrifyingly fast moves, my hands that had found the demons throat, felt for the creature's spine and quickly severed the connection between the spine and the beast's brain. I felt the crack and rip of the creature's neck as my hands tore into it and watched then as the creature fell at my feet in a pile of skin, muscle, and bones, and quickly, almost too quickly, it began to melt away into the earth.

First the skin, followed by the muscles, and finally the bone seemed to turn into sick black looking ooze that disappeared into the bowels of the earth underfoot. I stood alone now in shocked silence.

Starring at my feet where the most hideous creature imaginable had lay moments before. Realizing what I had just done, I stood there, mouth open, eyes wide, and arms hanging dead at my side. I stood frozen for unknown moments unable to move, but then something started to nag at me from the back of my mind. It was a rhythmic noise, loud and almost sharp. As my mind began to refocus, the noise got louder. And as I finally came back to reality from the daze inside my head, I realized that the noise was the sound of someone clapping.

At first nothing could be seen, only flittering movements and rough shapes dancing in the shadows. The only light available didn't seem to come from any directed place, but rather from all places at once. Yet it might have been better if no light existed at all, for this small amount only made it possible to see shadows and nothing more. It was just enough so your eyes could never adjust to the darkness. And yet it was that darkness that threatens to choke out all life in this barren and forsaken place, a place containing only stone, anger, and hate. In this land of nothing, there existed a sole mountain, jutting skyward from a barren and empty land. This mountain of foreboding stone had been carved out by the bare hands of the creatures exiled to this prison. Inside this hive of stone, shadows moved from room to room. Occasionally fights broke out, mostly from the boredom and the hate that grew in this silence. But for most of the time, nothing happened. Beasts moved about in the emptiness, some roamed the land, some sat for days at a time, others sparred or trained, all seemed to be waiting for something to occur. A main hall was situated in the center of the mountain, a room that took hundreds of clawed and powerful hands hundreds of years to scrape and shatter away stone in order to carve such a room from the pure rock of the mountain. Claw marks were visible on the walls and doors, evidence of the labor that went into creating such a structure. At the far back wall, a throne seemed to rise up out of the stone floor. On this rock sat a shadow of a man and from this thing pure evil emanated forth. The anger, hate, and pure rage seemed to tangibly pulse off of the being that reigned in this darkness. Around this throne many shapes skittered and trudged about in the blackness. The occasional guttural sound seemed to issue out of some corner, but other than that, silence consumed it all.

Then, almost suddenly, a small and pitch-black creature entered the main hall. The room was made up of solid rock and the small clicking of the creature's talons scraping across the hard stone was now the only audible sound. The thick and nearly impenetrable darkness pervaded everything and consumed all. Only the same faint, weak light could be seen, but it only shed a miniscule amount of visibility to the surroundings areas. A thick stench rose up and surrounded the small beast as it slithered into the hall. Massive forms seemed to rise and fall in the darkness just outside the small creature's eyesight. A gathering seemed to be taking place in this cold, dark palace. The little beast looked like a small monkey with a tail that was too long for its body and was subsequently lifted straight into the air behind it. The tail was extremely menacing and powerfully built, but the rest of the beast looked weak in comparison. Several pairs of glowing yellow eyes lifted and peered at the small intruder as it ventured deeper into the hall.

"*Master?*" A whining and pitiful sound rang out from the throat of the small creature into the darkness settling the prior movement as all eyes focused on the source of the noise.

"*Yes, Slythin.*" A cruel and powerful voice replied, "*What do you have for me?*"

The whining from the cowering beast continued, "*Gorganth has not returned from his mission, My Lord.*" The beast cowered even further at this point, shrinking back from the wrath of the thing he addressed. "*He was k...killed, Sire.*"

"*What!*" roared the powerful voice, "*Killed?*"

And suddenly a quick and dominant hand thrust out of the surrounding darkness and enclosed the small creature's neck. With one smooth motion the monkey-like beast was lifted into the air and held aloft in front of the eyes of the other creatures in the room. With a voice full of anger and loathing the powerful being began to speak anew.

"*So it has begun. The war for the earth has now been set in motion. The enemy has chosen a warrior and I...I will crush the life out of him.*"

And with that final remark the powerful hand flexed and the sounds of cracking bones could be heard over the screams of terror that broke out from the mouth of the writhing beast. The crushed and broken creature was tossed idly to the side and soon after that, all which could be heard penetrating the thick and merciless darkness was a cruel and hateful laugh.

As reality came swimming back, I looked over to my right, toward the direction the sound was coming from. I saw nothing at first, and then a man stepped out from under the shadow of a nearby tree. But this was no normal man. He had to be seven feet tall. Enormous. And not just tall mind you. He was built. He looked like some warrior barbarian from a distant past. He was clothed in what looked like robes, but they seemed to be plain and rather boring. In fact, I expected to see some huge double-bladed ax hung over his shoulders but the man didn't seem to carry any weapon at all. The giant was looking directly at me and he was slowly clapping.

"Well don't just stand there gaping at me Lad. Come over here and let me get a good look at you."

I didn't move, still too stunned from the past fight and way too confused to now approach a seven-foot barbarian. The giant man laughed and started toward me. I jumped back reactively, still feeling the energy and fight that had built up inside of me.

"Now, now, come on Lad. There is not so much time left for fooling around. We best leave this place quickly; the local residents are getting a bit flustered."

As the giant said this I looked around. He was right, the families must have heard or seen my fight and some were now coming out to investigate the noises. After that, the giant man started to walk away from me. He seemed nice enough, but I wasn't about to let my guard down yet, not after what I had just seen. After a few steps the man turned and beckoned for me to follow. Some of the residents were starting to come over to me, so I smiled sheepishly at them and jogged down the path after the giant. I caught up to him after a few paces and slowed down so we could walk nearly side by side. I wasn't going to get too close yet.

"That was some fight you just had, wouldn't you agree?"

I looked up at the man stupidly, not really knowing what to say. The big man laughed again and continued.

"That was one of the lesser demons," he said, "but pretty nasty for a first fight, if I do say so myself. But Boy you handled yourself quite well. I thought the beast had you when you got knocked one. But I see now that you are much more than you seem to be. Am I right?"

I still didn't know what to say, so I just nodded my head, never taking my eyes off the big man next to me. Finally he stopped walking and turned to face me. This man was bigger than any other man I had ever seen and so massive too. He appeared to be more than a match for the demon thing I had just fought.

"All right, I guess its time for introductions. My name is Ronoh. And you my friend, you must be Trans."

The big man laughed again and extended a powerful and massive hand. I weakly extended my own to match his. His hand fully enveloped mine and I felt just a hint of his strength as he gently squeezed and let go.

"Now we should get walking again," he continued, "it would be no good if the neighbors saw you standing here and talking with yourself. They can see me just as well as they could see that creature you killed back there."

And with that he turned and walked off again. Now my attention was back, along with my questions and intellect. I quickly ran and caught up.

"You mean that thing back there was invisible? What did the witnesses think I was doing, flying through the air by myself?"

More questions wanted to spring forth and might have if Ronoh hadn't raised his hand, demanding silence.

"I know you have a lot of questions; that is partly why I was sent to you. But you will just have to wait until we get somewhere where you will not be overheard, because they can't hear me at all and a young boy yelling at the air might look a little suspicious."

So we walked on in complete silence, side by side. If anyone could see us together, we made quite the odd couple. A gigantic man and a lanky teenager, but I guess a man of his size would attract attention anywhere. So we walked for about fifteen minutes until we found a secluded place and sat down on a bench. Exhaustion had begun to catch up with me. That energy I had absorbed was leaving and taking a lot of my strength with it. The giant stranger was silent for a few minutes. I sat unthinking, staring off ahead of me and back into the profile of this mysterious man. After several minutes he finally broke the silence.

"I know your mind is racing right now, I can sense it. I know you have hundreds of questions and are rightfully confused about, well, pretty much everything. But before you open up and explode at me with all of your thoughts, let me tell you a story first. Then we can see about your questions."

Ronoh was right, I was really confused, but I shook my head weakly at the giant's request, feeling too confused, tired, and small to voice my own opinion.

"Let me take you back to the beginning, if you'll let me?" Ronoh placed one mighty hand upon my shoulder and looked into my eyes. "This may be a little weird at first."

Enter Illiathat

Before I found the words to reply, my eyesight darkened into blackness and I heard Ronoh's voice ring out inside my head.

He sighed, "It all started back in the time you might call the dark ages. It was a time of chivalry, honor, pride, and fierce wars. What you experienced today with that creature was an aftereffect of what took place back then. There existed many feuding households in those days, royal families working hard to establish strong and powerful kingdoms, to gain followers and warriors."

As Ronoh spoke images began to flash before my mind's eye. My head reeled at the realization of what was occurring. I was actually going to see the events that took place.

Ronoh continued. "Wars broke out among the different lands as the different families strove to conquer others in an attempt to take their land and their wealth. As these families grew in size and consumed the land around them they naturally grew larger, gained more power, and eventually became small kingdoms. Many in due course found ways to coexist, to live in peace with one another, establish trade, and prosper together. Sadly others strove only for domination. At one point the existing peaceful kingdoms formed a massive alliance, joining together their forces and forming substantial armies. These armies were now capable of insuring peace for the surrounding areas. Their manpower alone caused the warring kingdoms to lay down their arms and submit. This trend and lifestyle continued for years. But all that time, there was one family that was never content.

They were known as the House of Deteath, led by a powerful king, one whose only desire was ultimate power and control. He thrived on death and destruction. This new alliance angered him to such a degree that he vowed to do anything he could to destroy it. At first he sent messengers to all the neighboring kingdoms and the lands beyond, seeking any form of alliance that would give him the upper hand. For although his kingdom was formidable and his men fierce, they would have been overrun by the colossal army of the Alliance. But, his messengers returned unsuccessful. His plea for help toward the destruction of the Alliance was rejected unanimously. Some messengers even came back with threats against his kingdom for even thinking of such an act. This final straw drove the king nearly insane; he beheaded all the messengers publicly for their failures and then decided to seek other methods for achieving his goal. This twisted and corrupt obsession led the king into the dark arts and the king eventually started to experiment with the spirit realm.

He was unsuccessful at first. But slowly the spirit world began to give him its attention. He began to sacrifice his men to please these creatures he called upon. For the blood of these men, the king asked and began to receive, an increase in strength, speed, and agility. He desired anything that would make him a better fighter. He began to get stronger and faster, up to the point of invincibility. The king began sacrificing women and then children, anything to increase his powers

31

beyond what it had become. The king became nearly unstoppable in combat. Even whole groups of men could not take him down. He was preparing to go out into war, to wage a battle against the Alliance, relying solely on the strength he alone possessed. That was when the creature known as Illiathat came to him.

He first appeared as a servant, one who has come only to please and fulfill the wishes of his master, the king. He persuaded the king not to declare war just yet, for although he was nearly unstoppable in battle, his men would be cut down fast by the numerous armies of the Alliance. So the king took heed of Illiathat's warnings, listening to the seemingly sound advice of this new counselor. But the king would be soon deceived, for Illiathat is a prince of lies. He told the king that there was a way to increase the power of his men and it would not require a huge sacrifice.

"All it would be," hissed the creature *"is a simple merging."*

He told the king that his men would become unstoppable killing machines, that his new army would no longer require food or sleep, and would be obedient to no one but the king. The men would have strength and power unmatched throughout all of time, capable of destroying anything in their way, an army of immeasurable force.

"But," whispered Illiathat with a hiss, *"it would of course, have to be voluntary."*

The king was delighted. He called for the gathering of his army. The men arrived forming battalions thousands deep. The king stood before them, high on the rampart walls, and called out to his loyal subjects, his loud voice echoing of the stone ramparts, telling the men of their choice that was to come. They marveled at the king's newfound strength and reveled in the thought of finally putting an end to the cursed Alliance and, above all else, having the power and strength they saw in their king, as their own. As the king made his persuasive request nearly all of his men stepped forward to accept it, unaware of the terror that would await them. Upon the king's command, the men of the army instantly slaughtered the few that didn't move. Suddenly the king made all his men take a knee and slowly he began the incantation. The men soon took it up as they began to follow the words and sounds he spoke. They called upon the demon lords in a language long forgotten and feared, asking, begging to be given the gifts they thought were coming. And come they did.

Slowly the sky above the men seemed to rip and tear open as if a jagged knife had been drawn violently across the azure above. It appeared to open into blackness, a darkness that threatened to consume them all. The men began to stare with wide, terrified eyes and all gave up the chant they had begun. The king alone continued the chant he had started. Hurriedly, strange and ghost-like shapes began to twirl and twist away from the opening. They appeared substance-less as they spun and flew out into the open air. Thousands of these spirits seemed to flee from the opening before it finally began to be pulled shut by some unseen force. The air above the army was full of spinning and fluttering phantasms. Then, almost casually, the shapes began to tumble down toward the army below. Unexpectedly and with a speed and an unearthly scream the ghosts descended on the now terrified army, most of who had fallen to the ground horrified.

The king looked greedily down on his people as the spirits entered into the men, most started to writhe on the ground, foaming at the mouth and screaming incoherently out into the cold air, apparently facing unbearable torture at the invisible hands of some ancient enemy. Soon all the spirits had disappeared and entered into their new bodies. All that is, but one. Illiathat, the demon lord, stood behind the now grinning king, grinning as well. And as the army below began to stand back up and fill in the ranks once more, the demon lord stepped forward to claim the body of the king. The once powerful lord drew in a sharp breath as the demon he thought served him alone forced his way into his body. The king felt himself lose control. He felt his consciousness being ripped away as he fell backward into darkness, falling into the echoes of his own screams. When Illiathat opened his eyes he found that he was no longer looking out into the world through the eyes of the spirit, he was now gazing upon thousands of his own kind, his new army of once-men, through the eyes of the flesh. Illiathat was king.

I sat back as I tried to gather in all the images and thoughts that had flashed and danced before my eyes. Confusion threatened to overcome my mind, but before it had its chance, a feeling of peace overtook it and new images began to appear. Ronoh continued to talk.

"At once the king ordered a full-out assault against the neighboring kingdoms. The army of once-men swept out of the castle grounds and marched onward toward the opposing settlements. King Illiathat led them. The massive army quickly overran the surrounding areas, destroying all property and killing everyone in their path. These once-men didn't stop at men though; they killed anything that moved from cattle to women and children. They showed no mercy as they swept through the villages and towns.

As soon as word reached the Alliance that the kingdom of Deteath was on the march, the whole of the might of the Alliance was raised up in preparation for the coming battle. And as the army of Deteath, led by the invincible Illiathat reached the main kingdoms of the Alliance, an army dwarfing that of the House of Deteath stood assembled before them. The Alliance out numbered the Kingdom of Deteath five to one. But, the Alliance was doomed to be routed, the armies and the remaining men were doomed to be scattered, and Illiathat would reign supreme. While the army of the Alliance was made up of men, the House of Deteath's army consisted of something more. These once-men were too powerful and moved with a speed and a quickness that was unmatched by even the finest fighters of the Alliance. Yet even this speed and strength would have proved insufficient to the sheer numbers of the Alliance. Still, somehow Illiathat's army succeeded. They did so because they had yet another advantage. These once-men had impenetrable skin. The steel of the Alliance had no power over Illiathat and his once-men. The men of the Alliance could not pierce the skin of their enemy. So as the battle raged on, the army of once-men didn't lose a single man. Yet, even against such terrifying and one-sided odds, the Alliance battled on."

As the giant retold this story to me, the images came rapidly to my mind. I saw Illiathat take the body of the King of the House of Deteath. I saw the army of once-men march on the towns and villages

35

and I saw the following destruction of life. I saw the might of the Alliance gather and stand their ground against the coming invincible horde. I saw how the once-men laughed as they tore through the lines of the Alliance. I watched as arrows bounced off the skin of once-men. How swords that ought to have removed the head of a man, would only slice across the neck, leaving the once-man unhurt. I saw the stunned faces of the Alliance as their brethren were slaughtered and yet they still fought valiantly on. And at last I saw the few remaining men that once made up the proud and mighty army of the Alliance, turn and run. After that, darkness clouded my sight and Ronoh began to speak once more.

"There were some that could kill these once-men." Ronoh began, "Even Illiathat at the time would not face these men alone. They were a group known simply as Paladins. These men were both powerful and righteous, men who gave their lives over to the light and swore to protect it and the lives of others, no matter the cost. These men were more than a match for any of the once-men of Illiathat's army. Yet, they numbered almost one thousand and were scattered widely throughout the land"

"But," Ronoh continued, "They did exist and they pledged to rid the land of this fierce foe. As the once-men, led by Illiathat, raided the land, destroying life and property, the Paladins gathered and devised a way to stop them. The once-men were wary of the Paladins and stopped traveling alone since a few of them found their paths crossed by one and never returned home. Of all the men hated by Illiathat and his once-men, the Paladins were the most feared. For these few men could cause death to the near invincible army of darkness, and with death the Paladins brought fear to Illiathat. So the Paladins came together and created a plan of attack that would be simple. The Paladins would not fight a war with force, knowing full well that any all-out confrontation would result in the massacre of the Paladins, for even though they were fierce fighters and more than a match for any once-man, the numbers of Illiathat's army would prove the difference. So they determined to fight this war as their Lord had years ago. They decided to end Illiathat's reign through a sacrifice."

As Ronoh said these last words the images came again. I saw the mighty Paladins assemble, and with them the priests, clerics, monks, and freemen who escaped the army of once-men so far. I saw them settle on their fate and send messengers to Illiathat. The Paladins would call him out. They openly declared war on Illiathat and his entire army. They said they would gather and face them in the Valley of Shadows. Illiathat laughed at the message, beheaded the messenger, and sent a member of his once-men to return with the head and the reply that the challenge would be accepted.

The next image came clearly into my mind. It showed the Valley of Shadows. On one side, an army of nearly a thousand Paladins assembled, massive men, all heavily armored and each wielding giant weapons. Most gripped huge broadswords in one giant arm, while holding an equally giant shield with the other. Symbols of a cross adorned them all. Others held maces of colossal size. Equipped with ferocious spikes and hooks attached to the massive heads. One man stood in the front, the obvious leader. He easily dwarfed the next largest man. He appeared to be as big as Ronoh himself. He held in one hand a mace that was nearly six feet long. Yet his was different. It had blocks at both ends, with viciously sharp spikes jutting forth from all sides. The lead Paladin stood out a step ahead of his men. His strong and commanding face hardened with thoughts of the coming battle. Across from him the army of Illiathat gathered.

They arrived in full force, determined to kill every being that opposed them. Illiathat stood in the back, watching from atop the valley's rim. When the commanding Paladin saw that the once-men had come in full force a slight smile spread across his face. With an inhuman roar Illiathat ordered his men to attack and with a reply that nearly deafened the Paladins, the once-men charged across the valley floor. In view of the coming devastation and death, the Paladins held their ground, waiting until the last possible minute to defend themselves. With screams of hate and rage the once-men came on, ignorant of their surroundings, obsessed with only the thought of the kill. As they reached the earth twenty yards before the Paladins the ground gave way before the coming onslaught. The once-men fell heedlessly into a thick muddy trench, too deep to stand. With the trap sprung and with the beasts slowly wading through the thick and binding mud, the Paladins rushed to meet them. The Paladins attacked with such fervor that the first wave of once-men were killed as they sloshed through the mud. But the creatures behind stepped and trampled on their fellow fighters, delirious with hate, bent only on the death of their enemies. The Paladins where soon driven back. The once-men had taken a massive toll, but were still too numerous for the heroic Paladins.

Then from nowhere the massive Paladin from the front showed up. He swung his giant mace at the onrushing once-men, crushing the chests and heads of the creatures with his mighty weapon. His war cry rang clear and powerful as he cut a wide path through the shocked army. Not used to having to defend themselves from fatal attacks, the once-men fell back and began to panic. Instantly the warring parties separated and Illiathat himself stepped forward to meet the substantial Paladin. As the two armies stepped back and faced each other the future outcome was clearly visible, for although the Paladins had caused massive losses to the once-men, they too had suffered. Their number was reduced to something around two hundred, while Illiathat and his men still had thousands. With a powerful cry the lead Paladin roared, "Now!" and rushed to meet Illiathat. The sword of the king demon was curved like an "S" and serrated on one side. He held it aloft with one arm as the mighty mace came forward with a blow that should have cleaved the demon lord's arm from his body. Instead the mace rang off as metal struck metal and Illiathat smiled. The massive Paladin continued his ruthless assault on the demon king, each time being repulsed by merely a wave of the demon's sword. As the fight wore on, cloaked and robbed figures began to appear around the edges of the valley. The demon fighters below were unaware as they hungered for the death of these men that could cause them harm. As the numbers of men grew around the valley it became clear that the men were praying. Soon the arms of these robed men began to rise till all of them were lifted skyward, and suddenly a soft chant began. It was picked up by every figure that circled the valley. Illiathat and his once-men still ignored the newcomers, unaware of their presence as they prepared for the coming slaughter. As the chant grew louder the lead Paladin began to grow clearly tired, he stumbled as he dodged a blow sent forth by Illiathat and as he fell he raised his powerful mace in a desperate attempt to ward off the coming deathblow. Illiathat's weapon sliced downward, cutting the Paladin's weapon in half and was quickly followed with a slice to the brave warrior's throat. As the giant fighter slid to the ground, holding the wound as blood issued forth from the fatal strike, a faint smile was again visible on his face.

With the lead Paladin's demise the remaining once-men charged forward again, caught up in the frenzy of death, eager to feel the blood of the men before them. The remaining Paladins, faces hardened with their coming death, fought valiantly to the end. As the once-men roared past Illiathat to the anticipated slaughter, the lord's his eyes turned upward to the valley's ridges, becoming suddenly aware of the men in robes. His mind froze as he heard their chant rise in strength. For the first time in the existence of Illiathat's being he felt fear.

The chant rose higher and higher, filling the valley, shaking the heavens. In an instant, as the remaining Paladins struggled for life, the space around the whole valley seemed to rip and tear open. As the last Paladin fell to the sword of a once-man, the rip spread out across the whole valley floor, engulfing the entire army. Then, in the instant the rip covered all the beings in the valley, it closed. Sealing up the rift into the nothingness it came from and taking with it all the creatures in the valley below. A wild cheer went up from the men standing around the valley. Many fell to their knees lifting songs and praise to the heavens. Then my vision again went black and with that came the return of Ronoh's voice.

"So now you see," he continued, "Now you know what is happening, what must be done."

"What!" I exclaimed. "See what! How does this affect me? What is happening to me?" I exploded. I would have continued on with this rant had it not been for Ronoh again and the slight rise of his hand.

"Listen. Illiathat and his army were banished back into the spiritual realm." Ronoh said calmly, "The prayers, the faith of the Paladins, and the faith of the people were enough to achieve this goal. For a time the threat had ended. But now things are changing. The rift that once held these creatures back is tearing." Ronoh looked at me now and I could see sadness and a deep weariness in his eyes as he went on. "Faith is dying Trans. People are forgetting the truth, ignoring God, and turning their backs on grace. This is causing the rift to weaken and is giving Illiathat a chance to send his weaker subjects back into this world."

"But," I interrupted, "I thought you said these creatures looked like men. That thing I killed looked nothing like a man to me."

"Yes, "replied Ronoh, "things have changed for Illiathat too. At one time all these creatures looked like men. But they have been contained inside a place of nothingness. Think of a realm that had only enough light to make it seem like midnight on the darkest night

41

imaginable. A realm where nothing lives, a cold place made solely of stone and darkness. That is where these creatures were exiled. There they changed. Some took on forms like the creature you saw before, all muscle and strength, a fighter. Others became more insect-like. Still others grew bigger for strength, or smaller for speed, but all deadly and now, invisible to everyone. These once-men have become nothing less than demons fitted and equipped with flesh. And," Ronoh ended, "it is your job to destroy them."

For a while I stared blankly into the eyes of the huge man before me, millions of thoughts racing and dancing through my head. After a while I ripped my gaze away from his and looked off into the foreground. I was at a loss. My mind reeled with this newfound information. The impossibility of it all struck me dumb. How was I to fight thousands of demons? Creatures that could destroy armies five times their size and whose skin was impenetrable to iron. But I was not just tormented by those thoughts alone. Others terrified me even more. These things were not human. They might have been at one time. But now, if I was to believe in what this stranger told me, these things were demons incarnate, led by one more powerful than anything I could imagine. I finally stammered out,

"But, I...I don't even believe in God."

With that remark a smile began to spread across the giant man's face. He almost seemed to laugh at me. He seemed to take on the air of a sympathetic parent, whose child had just said something ridiculous. Something that all adults know, but the child is yet to learn.

"Lad, do you remember what the thing you just killed looked like?"

I nodded dumbly. I knew I would never forget that image.

"Is there any doubt in your mind that that beast was anything other than a demon?"

Again, I consented. "But…" I stammered.

"But what?" The giant stranger added, seemingly a little annoyed. "Well, what do you think I am?"

With that question, I turned to look once again on my strange new acquaintance. His eyes met mine and seemed to shine forth like he and I both shared some form of merriment that caused a warm smile to stretch back into the man's face.

"Well…" he continued. "Here, maybe this will help."

With that he stood, threw back his shoulders and rose to his full height. The man was easily seven feet tall and massively proportioned, with a huge chest and equally impressive arms and legs. The giant threw back his head and began to sing. But the sound was nothing like a human voice, the notes resounding out from the giant before me where utterly amazing and breathtakingly beautiful. There were no words I could understand, but the music from this being was something that filled me with wonderment, strength, hope and love. As I sat listening to the beautifully sounding song a strange thing began to occur. The giant began to glow, faintly at first, then more brilliantly as the song elevated in strength and power. Finally I was forced to turn away as the light flowing forth from this stranger caused my eyes to ache. Finally after a moment longer, the light seemed to wane a little. I looked back and was stunned by the site. The man before me no longer stood in the same normal, plain robes he had on before. Instead the giant seemed to be wrapped in a loose fitting toga. One that stretched across his chest leaving his right arm exposed. The material he wore seemed to give off its own radiance. It was held at the waist by what looked like a strong, thick leather belt with a brilliant gold clasp in the front. From that belt hung a sword, one that from the man's waist hung almost to the floor. The man seemed to stand illuminated by some unseen and unknown light. He seemed to be light himself. As my eyes began to take in more of the sight before me, I realized this man was different in another way. This man...had wings. Not just small little bird wings either. But wings that raised a good three to four feet further up from his already massive shoulders and when he spread them out seemed to be all of fourteen feet in length. He looked at me then, a strange new power radiated outward from his being. One that terrified me more than the demon had before. This man was clearly more than a man. This creature before me was an angel, and the power of a real God flowing out from this being made me fall to my knees in shock and in fear. I closed my eyes from the light, but I felt it invade my being unopposed. I felt exposed and naked before the glory presented before me. The idea of a real God, all-powerful and magnificent scared me to death. I tried to shrink lower, to hide from that idea and that penetrating light. But all I could do was let the light invade me and expose me. After several minutes the feelings began to subside. I felt my surroundings come back, my senses realign. I felt normal once more. After another moment I opened my eyes to again face the being before me. But Ronoh was no longer standing in front of me. I felt a moment of panic begin to rise from my gut. I was alone again. I slowly got up off my knees and realized that the angel had not left my side, but rather had re-seated himself down next to me on the park bench.

"I...I don't know." I finished there. I had nothing else to say. I shook my head in wonderment of what had just happened today. The thoughts of all the events of today and what led up to the present rushed and crashed together in my mind. I was completely overwhelmed, and the tears came. I put my head into my hands and cried. Not for any particular reason, but solely out of confusion from the past events. I felt the massive hand of Ronoh settle onto my shoulder and my back. And from that touch a feeling of pure relaxation and peace flooded my mind, freeing it of the thoughts that tormented it.

"I know it is a lot to take in, Son, but that is why I was sent. I am to guide you and aid you with all the power God has granted unto me." I looked once again into the eyes of the being next to me and images of hope, sadness, and power reflected back into mine.

"Why me?" I managed to stutter out. "Why am I chosen for this? What makes me so special? Till this day," I said with a little confusion, "I didn't even know God existed." I hung my head down, and looked into the ground.

"Well Lad, I would think it was quite obvious." With that I looked back up, surely this creature was having fun with me. Nothing could have been more obscure than the answer I sought. But the angel meant no jest. When I looked back into his face, I saw the hint of a smile and pure joy mirrored in his eyes. He must have registered the shock on my face, because he gave a slight laugh.

"What could possibly be so funny?" I nearly shouted.

"Calm down, calm down." He reassured me. "Your heart Son, your heart." I must have still looked a little confused, for the angel continued.

"Lad, you have a pure heart. You have been given a clear image of right and wrong. You can see life clearer and judge what is right with more purity with the help and the strength of God. It doesn't matter if you didn't believe God existed before now, your actions were still right, your heart still moved and pushed toward righteousness. Whether or not you knew it, God was working in you right from the beginning, and he will continue his work to completion."

"Completion!" I replied, "What more could He want with me?"

Ronoh looked at me again and with power in his voice answered, "Want with you? That's an easy one; He wants nothing less than all of you."

"So…So now what? What do I do now? Do I just go and attack the invisible army of Illiathat or whatever? Just walk right up to thousands of demons and start hitting them? What…"

"Slow down, Son." Ronoh interjected, "Everything will be explained in good time. Right now I had to start by introducing you to the whole plan. Details will come with time."

I stared once again into the face of this angel. Confusion, anger, fear, and a thousand other feelings and emotions swirled and danced in my mind. Questions unanswered, fears unrelieved.

"Well," Ronoh replied, "I really must be going soon, people to see you know?" He stood with a chuckle.

"No...No I don't know," I said with a little too much anxiety in my voice, "What am I supposed to do?"

"Right now, go home; see your family, rest. Tomorrow go to school, continue on with life. For a time is approaching fast, when your life will change forever. This here is only the beginning. See you soon Lad."

And with that he was gone. The angel disappeared and I was left staring off into the sky. After several minutes of delay and confusion I got an unsure grasp on my mind, enough where I could begin to walk and with that, I headed home.

Ronoh, captain of the Host of Heaven, looked out after the departing boy and was met by two companions. One of them began to address their captain.

"He did well, Sir."

"Yes, Trevol, he did." Replied Ronoh, "But that was a minor demon. There will be others who could defeat him."

47

Here the other angel spoke, "But you can train him right? You could strengthen him."

"I can only do so much. Free will. If he chooses to give himself up and over to God he will be able to do amazing things."

Trevol picked up, "But is he strong enough to defeat Illiathat?"

"Not yet," said Ronoh, "But he could be… and by the grace of God he will be."

Training Day

That night was a mixture of emotions. I had dinner with my family, hung out a little with my sister and my parents, rolled around with my dogs, and watched a little TV. My thoughts danced and collided in my mind all night, so I felt a little out of it socially with my family. But no one said anything, so I don't know if I was too obvious or not. I tried to go to bed that night, but nightmares ruled my dreams and I awoke a few times, sweating, with a racing pulse. When my alarm went off in the morning I had hardly slept a wink and I felt like absolute crap. I staggered from my bed to the shower, from the shower to breakfast, and from there, to school. I looked and felt dead. Some people could tell something was up and a few of them even went out of their way to ask me what was going on. I just shrugged off their questions and changed the subject. They would never understand.

From my first meeting with Ronoh things in my head had changed. I knew what was expected of me. I knew what I had to do. These demons were killing people and I had to stop them at any cost. I understood that thought in the foundation of my being.

It was a foundation I held onto as the rest of my soul was uprooted and changed by the appearance of Ronoh and my newfound abilities. Ronoh began making more and more frequent visits. Most times we talked about God, my abilities, and life. Ronoh began to become a truly good friend and counselor. He seemed to understand my feelings, my fears, and my anxieties. He was a strong and constant force of reassurance and guidance. My time with him continued to grow and at the same time I began to distance myself from everyone at school and at home. They knew something was wrong and when they talked to me I was always distant and remote. They eventually just stopped trying and rested instead on making comments and throwing taunts, which wasn't so much different than before. But through it all, I couldn't let the pain they tried to inflict deter me from my goal. I started to get made fun of a lot more and with much more frequency and intensity. Kids in school began to notice that I was becoming increasing more distant, remote, and generally "off." They began to see that I wouldn't reply to remarks and would just walk away. Because I was an easy target, some kids began to ridicule me more and more. My strange actions and reclusive nature only fueled these kids' resentment and confusion toward me. They began calling me a freak, weird, lame, and hundreds of other nicknames and taunts. I just walked away from that too.

Ronoh and I kept meeting. My parents began to wonder what was happening. Why I was distant and reclusive. I just told them I was going through a phase and I just needed my space. They said they understood but they continued to worry and to ask questions. They became extremely suspicious of my afternoons away from home. They knew I wasn't with the kids I used to tag along with, so they worried even more. They questioned me on everything from girls to drugs. How could I have told them I was spending time with an angel?

After a good chunk of time had passed and I was getting more and more accustomed to the ridicule that followed me, I found myself meeting with Ronoh again and curious about the demons I was supposed to be hunting. I realized I had been spending a lot of time with Ronoh, but that I hadn't had any strong urges like the first few. I asked if that meant the demons were not busy right now.

"On the contrary Trans," Ronoh began, "They have been quite busy. I have just been blocking the urges from you."

"What?" I yelled out frantically, "Why? Why would you do that? Are you telling me that people have been dying?"

Ronoh cut me off, as he has been so prone to do. "You were and are still not ready."

"I killed that one," I remarked, "What's your problem? The people?"

"You would have been killed, how good would you be if you were dead?"

"Killed, but I thought I was...was... invincible. That I only got stronger within a fight."

"Partly true, but there are creatures that are strong enough to kill you in one blow or many, before you could get any more strength, these have been active and you are still not ready to face demons of this kind."

I looked at my friend in shock, "What? Why didn't you tell me? Why keep it a secret? I could have trained. I could do something, couldn't I? Did all those people have to die?"

Ronoh looked at me and a faint smile mixed with sadness floated briefly across his strong and commanding face. "I'm sorry Trans, but you had to grow first, not in battle, but in heart and mind. You had to come to this place that you are in now. You had to recognize the need for you personally; you had to ask to begin your training. I was not sent to force you into action. I was sent to give you a choice."

"Train me then!" I exploded, "People have died because I wasn't ready. That will not happen anymore."

"You could lose your friends, your family, and possibly your life if you chose to take this path." Ronoh interjected, "Think carefully, it is a hard decision."

I looked down at my feet feeling the full blow this comment was supposed to make on my heart. Images of my friends and family passed before my eyes. But then I saw the victim's friends and their families.

"My decision is made." I said, "I will train and I will fight, no matter the cost." I met Ronoh's gaze and held it. A firm resolve strengthen in me as the words of my decision broke forth from my lips.

"You do have a good heart," Ronoh said, "So your training begins tomorrow."

And like that, he was gone. I wandered off home, ate, and fell into my bed, anxious for the coming day and despairing that I had already wasted so much time.

Tomorrow was Saturday so I had no school. I awoke and went down to make myself a quick bite to eat. After shoving down some toast and orange juice I told my parents I was going to go for a run and before they could reply I was out the door. I figured Ronoh would be able to find me so I started off sprinting. I felt my God-given ability kick in as new energy began to travel into my legs and flow throughout my body. I started to run faster, taking bigger strides. I had so much nervous energy and hadn't exercised my powers for so long that I felt great joy in running. I started to jump in the midst of my run. My first few were impressive but with each impact on landing I began to jump higher and farther. Soon I was caught up in the rush. I started to jump higher than the houses in my neighborhood. I was foolish, it was early so no one was really out, but I'm sure a few people probably saw some person launching over houses some distance away. I came to a slamming and sliding halt as a roaring voice detonated into my head.

"Stop now!" The commanding voice sounded like a sonic boom, resounding and echoing in my head. I landed from a jump, fell, and rolled a few feet from the shock.

"You fool!" Echoed the same voice, "Are you so unaware of what you are?" Immediately Ronoh was in front of me, his massive form standing impressively before me.

"You are the possible destruction of the most terrifying demon to walk the earth. If he was to find out about you, he would send all possible demons immediately and they would kill you, your family, and anyone else you care about. You would be able to do nothing to stop them. You are not ready!"

With this last blast from Ronoh my face dropped and I felt waves of embarrassment and pride swell inside of me. I felt angry, red in the face, and I wanted to yell something right back into Ronoh's face. I looked up with that intent and met the eyes of my friend. They were nearly in tears. I dropped my face again. Now a new feeling poured out from my heart. I was ashamed at my reaction to his warnings. I felt my anger and bitterness slide away as I grasped true perceptive about my mistake. I looked back up and mumbled out an apology.

At that Ronoh smiled. "You are the right one for this job, Lad. I am thankful to be able to train you. Are you ready to begin?"

I looked up, nodded, and felt my resolve harden and prepare. I didn't know what was going to happen, but I wanted to be ready.

"Come with me then," Ronoh said, and with that he turned and began to run. At first I stood there, unsure of what to do, then as I saw Ronoh distancing himself from me, I took off after him. As we ran I felt myself getting faster but instead of gaining on the angel before me, Ronoh only seemed to keep getting further away. I tried to run faster but nothing seemed to work. The massive giant finally rounded a corner after a few miles and when I finally did the same he was nowhere to be seen. I stopped and collected myself. He has to be a little farther ahead. I looked around and found myself in the forest-like area that was left alone in the back of the suburban area I lived in. It was made up of sparse trees and tons of open space, but was equally well excluded from sight. I started to run again to see if he was ahead of me a little out of my range of sight. Then I stopped. Something registered in my mind. My training had begun and Ronoh would not catch me off guard. I dropped into a pathetic fighter's stance. I looked and felt clumsy but it was the best I could do. I started to look around. Trying to see where he could be hiding. Suddenly a stick snapped a few feet behind me. I whirled around quickly, arms raised in a defensive move to ward off my coming attacker. But nothing was there. The next thing I knew, a massive blow struck me in the middle of my back. It lifted me off the ground and seemed to throw me forward into a set of rock outcroppings that jutted out from the ground about twenty feet in front of me. I hit the rocks with a tremendous blow and shattered a few of the boulders I collided with. On top of that shock though, something else had happened, I was hurt. My nose was bleeding and the blow still stung in my back. It was the first time I had felt pain in a long time. As before I felt enormous amounts of energy flow into me, but pain was there this time as well. I began to get up, slipped, and finally stood. Ronoh was standing twenty feet from me; at the place he had hit me. He looked at me and sort of cocked his head in a questioning manner.

"You're a tough little guy now aren't you?" He said with confidence in his voice. "I wanted to knock you unconscious with the first blow. Guess I'll have to make it the second huh?"

As Ronoh was speaking I felt the pain beginning to ebb away. I thought I should keep him talking till it was all gone.

"You should have killed me, remember. Now I'm stronger."

"Do you think I hit you with everything I have? Interesting. That was merely a love tap. And you should have been ready. Did my little sound effect distract you?" And with that he smiled.

As I looked on at this massive warrior the last bit of pain subsided and the blood from my nose caked and fell away. I decided to play dumb. If he thought I was still hurt I had the advantage. I began to walk hunched over toward my trainer.

"My back hurts really badly still, is that normal?" I put my hand back onto it and seemed to be rubbing out the pain.

"Yes. I told you that you could be hurt, even killed if an enemy got to you before you had raised your energy enough." As the angel talked I was nearly five feet away and getting closer. I brought my energy up, feeling it open and pour into my blood and my body. As it all came rushing into me, I felt my muscles tighten and strengthen with the power of God. I continued to walk right up to Ronoh, pretending the lesson was over. It was far from over.

"As I said before," continued Ronoh, "You will learn new information with time...

I was nearly there...

"This training will help you considerably..."

I was right before my teacher. I looked up into his face with a look of pain and faked understanding. I yelled, pulled back my fist, and shot it forward with all the strength inside me. I felt it all gather into the punch I threw straight for Ronoh's face. But before my fist was halfway to its target, Ronoh's own collided with my chest. I felt myself being lifted off the ground again and thrown back. I felt a massive amount of energy fill me. More than I have ever felt before. But with that energy pain arrived as well, and lots of it. As I recoiled from the blow my body slammed back into the rocks. As I hit, stones exploded all around me, shattering and flying in a multitude of directions. I saw my vision begin to swim as darkness threatened to overcome my mind. But I fought it off with my heart, refusing to pass out. My head was swimming in such pain, more than I had ever felt in my life. It almost felt as if my chest would collapse. My breathing was shallow and quick and as I began to regain control of myself I heard Ronoh speak.

"First," he said, "keeping your opponent off-guard and unaware is good if you know the rules of the game. If not, than it is the quickest way to defeat. There are things you don't know which gave away your deceit in this instance. I can sense people's "energy levels," I guess one could call them. As you walked toward me and powered up I knew that you felt fine and were planning on attacking me. Second, you need to know your enemy before fighting. I have spent so much time working with you; I know what you are capable of. I knew that if I didn't knock you out, you would be fine in a matter of minutes. You on the other hand," he said with a smile, "don't know a thing about me. You don't know how fast I am, how strong, or how smart. You attacked without knowing and the consequences had I been a demon would have been your death. Learn from this now."

With that Ronoh extended his hand out to me to help me up. I grasped it with both of mine, but instead of pulling myself up I pulled him down. As a surprised look flickered across my mentor's face I pulled my knees to my chin and placed my feet on his chest. Before he could react I kicked outward and launched Ronoh up and out over the trees. He flew skyward at an amazing speed, but all of a sudden stopped in mid flight and slowly descended back to the place a few feet in front of me. I stared dumbfounded.

"So," he said casually, "you are a quick leaner I see. I didn't have to tell you anything and you already learned how to hide your energy levels. I am impressed and pleased. But you could have done worse things to me than launch me skyward." With that remark he laughed again.

I flipped up off the ground with quickness that by the look on Ronoh's face surprised even him.

"I just wanted you away for a sec, so I could catch my breath."

"Good," was his only reply. "Now, come at me."

With an awesome speed and tenacity I flew at my trainer. I attacked him high and low. I tried kicking, punching, and throwing but each attack was shunned, blocked and rejected. I started to get frustrated seeing all my attempts being thwarted. I tried harder, moving faster and quicker. Ronoh was still a step ahead of me. I finally jumped in with what appeared like an attempt to kick him and instead pushed off of his block with both feet and jumped about ten feet back. I paused to catch my breath. Even though throughout the fight I had gotten more energy, I was still unable to do any kind of damage. I looked at the warrior's face. He must have understood my look, because he started to talk.

"Your fighting form is unstructured and you leave much open after attacking." He said, "You need to try and sense your opponent instead of just attacking. The same is true when on defense. You are fast and extremely strong, but if you cannot prevent an attack against yourself you could be destroyed. For no matter how strong or fast you become, if you cannot stop an attacker he could impact horrendous damage on your body, enough that you might not be able to take it all in and transfer it to energy. You could be destroyed. Do you understand?"

I nodded, not really understanding at all.

"I'm going to come at you now." Ronoh continued, "Try and relax your mind and body. Feel for my attacks. Sense your surroundings, the change in my breathing, the slight turn in my body, and the change in the air as I begin to move. Look for these early signs and you will be much better off. Now prepare yourself." With that the angel pushed himself off the ground and flew straight for me.

As this powerful, God-sent being quickly began to close the gap between us I quieted my mind. I pushed out the screaming noise of fear, instinct, and thought. I forced my body and mind to relax, dropping slowly at the same time into a defensive stance, and brought my arms up in preparation. As Ronoh continued to gather speed he let out a massive roar and brought back his arm in one powerful and terrifying motion. I threw up my arms to block and instinctually flexed my power as I prepared to take on his massive attack. But right as Ronoh came within striking distance his figure seemed to blur and then disappeared. My mind almost panicked. I fought it back and then in the quiet of the back of my mind I felt it. Now…Behind!!! I spun around and ducked at the same instant. I felt a rush of wind as my trainer's powerful leg swung over my crouched position, barely missing my ducking head. In the few seconds I had before the sparing was to resume, I knew that the kick I dodged from this powerful angel would have knocked me out on contact.

I bounced right up into the angel's face and the true fight began. My counselor struck and attacked with a speed and cleverness I could never have imagined. My mind began to understand the attacks and I was able to block a few. But others made contact and struck me hard. Not enough to knock me down but enough to make me stumble back. Ronoh was clearly restraining himself. As the attack continued Ronoh gave me no room to breath or relax. Every time I fell back under his brutal attack he pressed it forward. I felt my power rising but the pain that came with it was certainly not worth it. As I got stronger I began to block his attacks with a little more success. Yet as I seemed to get better, Ronoh only seemed to get faster. As this training continued I knew I couldn't stand much longer. My body had been beaten more than I had ever been in my life. I knew that even though I was filled with an unbelievable amount of energy and strength, Ronoh was still stronger and that if nothing changed soon I was going to fall.

In an intense moment of frustration I decided I would no longer take any more punishment. I looked right into Ronoh's face as he landed another blow into my chest that rocked me backward. As he came forward to push his attack even further I struck out. I jumped up with my arm pulled back, a powerful yell bursting forth from my mouth, and as Ronoh lifted his arms to block my punch I struck out with my leg throwing all of my remaining strength behind it. I hit this powerful being dead in the chest with my kick, connecting right below his block. He flew backward under the force of my blow. I watched as this powerful angel, sent to train me, shattered a full-grown tree and then dug up a trough with his body as it slid back through the ground. I barely had the strength to stand now and looked at my friend and counselor who finally stopped moving about twenty feet from where I had hit him. As exhaustion threatened to overtake me I slumped down onto my knees. I was bloody, bruised, and exhausted. As my eyes began to close and darkness began to wrap its arms around my head, I saw Ronoh stand, brush the dirt and wood chips off of him and walk toward me, laughing and smiling. Then the blackness finally won and I collapsed into the earth and into the waiting arms of darkness.

I awoke after a while. Time was a concept I had no hold on for the moment. As sleep fell from my weary eyes I tried to sit up. My body protested loudly and I let out a soft moan as the soreness and pain inflicted on my body began to register in my mind.

"You awake?" Exclaimed my giant friend, "It's been a while and I was wondering when you might again bless me with your presence. We had a good first day of training, would you not agree?"

I raised my eyes to the giant angel who stood over my bruised and tattered body. All I could do was issue forth a faint smile through the pain I felt in my body.

"Good." said Ronoh, "Now get up and go home. Rest. We have many more days of this type of fun to prepare for."

With that statement I felt a massive hand reach out and take hold of my body. I was lifted almost effortlessly and placed on my feet. My body fought back powerfully against the idea of being on its feet again, but for the time being I was supported by Ronoh.

"Come on." He continued, "You need to move a little. Get the juices flowing again."

"So tired." Were the only two words I felt fall from my mouth.

"I know. I know. You did well, Lad. That last blow knocked me a good one. I haven't been hit like that in a long time. It felt pretty good. Now come on, walk with me."

I started to take a few steps and stumbled. Ronoh caught me and held me up again and after a few supported steps, I began to feel my body heal, slowly. After a few more feet I was walking by myself again and soon after the pain began to disappear altogether.

"See," exclaimed Ronoh, "all you needed was a little push. Your mind and body are amazing gifts. All you need to do is open the door and God can do amazing things through you. Never forget that. That is the key to the eventual defeat of Illiathat."

And with those remaining words I headed off for home with my giant, angelic companion. At some point as I trudged weakly home I noticed I was once again alone. Ronoh was gone but I knew he wasn't going to be gone for long. Tomorrow was another day and more than likely more training.

I got home and my parents questioned me, like they have got in the habit of doing, by asking me where I had been. I mumbled something about working out and escaped to my room. As soon as my head hit the pillow I was out and welcomed the soft touch of sleep. Morning seemed an eternity away and came just as slowly. I awoke feeling refreshed and vibrant. It was Sunday and the sun woke me up early. I looked out my window at the glorious sun as it began its slow and arduous journey through the sky. Looking at the world I decided to do something I had never done before. I decided to go to church. I figured if I was going to be doing some fighting for this all-powerful God I had better get to know him better first.

I found a church some kids from my school went to. I went and sat in the back and listened to the pastor speak. Something struck me there as I looked out into the chapel, looking around at the faces in the crowd. Some people were listening while others seemed to be falling asleep. Some people sang loudly and raised their hands when the group began worship. Others closed their eyes and quietly mouthed the words, singing a glorious melody to their personal God inside their heads. Still others looked embittered, angry at having to be in this place of God. Something else clicked then for me. Each of these people has their own view of what God is to them; of whom this mysterious Being is or should be. But none of them, including myself could ever know the splendor or greatness or true reality of what God is. I sat in awe as the power and all that is God overwhelmed my senses. As I stared out over this group I felt the fullness of the love that God has for these people on earth. I saw God's heart for man and His pain as some rejected his love. Tears filled my eyes as for the first time in my life I actually felt the love of Christ enter my heart. Then, almost naturally, I prayed. I prayed for forgiveness for my many faults. I prayed for redemption, for grace, for love. I prayed for the people in this church, for the people in my school, for my family, and my friends. I prayed against Illiathat and his demons and I prayed for the strength to defeat them. Finally, after that moment, a moment that felt like a lifetime, I opened my eyes. I felt a firm hand clasp down on my shoulder.

"I knew you were behind me." I said slowly, "I sensed your presence when I first walked in here." I turned on these words and looked at my mentor.

"Are you prepared?" Were the only words in Ronoh's reply.

I nodded and I walked forth from this house of the Lord and began another day of training.

From that day on I trained everyday. School, family, and life seemed to pass me by. I vaguely remember going to class. All of my waking moments were spent training and those that were not, became to me, merely periods of time known as "before training" and "after." During the day I would prepare my mind, mentally practicing moves and ideas. After practice I would pick up my tired body and drag it home to bed. My parents became used to my schedule, although they still questioned and pestered me. My sister thought I was doing drugs and started to ignore me. I was an outsider now more than ever. Some nights the feelings and the pain of being rejected was too much and I felt hot tears sting my eyes as I tried to find sleep. I awoke as usual and got back to my training though. God gave me the strength to move on. Life continued on like this for many days. All spent in training and thought. Till one day my life changed yet again.

"*Sir!*" Interjected a rather large and powerful demon, "*Our troops have not been attacked for some time. Maybe the death of Gorganth was a mistake.*"

"*Fool,*" replied Illiathat, "*there was no mistake. The enemy is trying to trick us again. Remember the Paladins.*"

After that thought Illiathat's brow furrowed in concentration and reflection.

"*Continue with the attacks. We need more blood. I almost have enough power to fully destroy this accursed rift and then nothing the enemy can do can stop me. Keep the patrols in groups. Find the identity of this mystery warrior. I want his name. Then destroy his family and his home. I want this fighter attacked from all sides. Make him angry and vengeful, and then we will have him. Understand?*"

The creature bowed low in respect toward the commands of his lord. With those departing words the beast stalked out of the palace to relay the orders and renew the attacks.

The True Test

This day began like all the others. I awoke after a painful day of training, refreshed and physically prepared for the coming activities. Sleep certainly helped in my healing process. I watched as school flew by and prepared for the coming day of training. Throughout all my lessons I had learned many new things. Ronoh guided me in different styles of fight. He taught me different stances and moves for attacking and defending. I learned how to use my ability to my greatest advantage. When I should take a blow to maximize the energy I would receive and when to dodge. I was taught how and where to attack in order to inflict the most damage on an opponent. But most importantly, I learned to use my mind to fight more than my body. I arrived at the forest area after school a little early and was confused to not find Ronoh waiting. Everyday my friend and mentor had been there prepared with new lessons to train me with, but not today. I called out and received no answer. Confusion and doubt taunted my mind. I turned in a circle looking every which way for my trainer, but to no avail. Then, in the shadows, I saw him standing under a tree. I walked up and stood before him.

"Well?" I said.

"It is time, Lad." Ronoh looked at me after these words and his face showed the slightest bit of sadness, which quickly fell away.

"Time for what?" I replied, "Time to fight?"

"Yes and no." were my teacher's answers. "You are as prepared as I can make you. But the true test for you will begin soon."

"I am ready." I said with bravado and a touch of cockiness in my voice.

"Are you?" Replied Ronoh rather harshly. "For Illiathat will not just attack your strength. He is a cunning and vicious opponent. He will strike at you from every direction he can. He is a dangerous enemy."

As Ronoh spoke something clicked again in my mind, "You fought him before, didn't you?" I commented. "That's why you were sent to train me. You know his strategy the best."

With that remark I saw Ronoh's eyes alight and blaze with power and anger. "Yes. Illiathat and I met in battle before. I was chosen to lead the attack against the demons summoned forth by the king of Deteath." Here Ronoh's voice seemed to waver. "It was my job to stop them from entering into your world. I failed and many of my angels were destroyed that day."

"It was not your fault." I nearly shouted. "Man's faith was weak. You showed me those images yourself."

Ronoh changed the subject. "Enough of the past. The future is what I am concerned with now. Illiathat must now be stopped for the rift is weakening and soon the whole army of Illiathat will be free. The lives of many men have been taken by the pawns of this dark king and soon enough energy will be stolen. Enough to allow Illiathat to break the bars that have imprisoned him in darkness and then all shall be lost."

I nodded and tried to look as brave as I could. But inside I was terrified of the coming battle.

Ronoh continued, "It is up to you now. You, Trans, must not allow any more lives to be taken into Illiathat's realm. The fate of the world depends on you. If the demons taste freedom again all could be lost."

I stared dumbly at the ground as the weight of this new responsibility fell onto my shoulders. I felt the weight of the earth try to crush me downward into the ground. But, somehow I still stood.

"Now," said Ronoh, "I must warn you of something else. As you travel and fight the demons of Illiathat you must not let any demons escape you. For Illiathat knows you exist. He has felt the power of God in you ever since your first kill and he is waiting to catch you off guard. If he discovers who you are it could mean death and destruction for you and everyone you hold dear. Do you understand?"

I again nodded. "Yes I do. But I have a question for you now?" Ronoh's eyes looked into mine and asked me to continue. "Why don't you help me? Can't you help? I mean you are an angel of God. Aren't there more like you? Couldn't you fight too?"

Ronoh just looked at me as I stammered out the questions that had been burning in my chest ever since I began to train. "Yes," he said, "myself and other angels like me could help. But for the moment Illiathat is unaware that angels have the ability to strike down these once-men. And although that is an advantage, I am afraid we are also much weaker than any of these once-men. For they are made of demon and flesh and as God has given man over to himself and his lusts, for now, those beings are much more powerful than any angel of God. That is why you, a human, have been chosen."

"B…But," I stammered out, "You've been training me, hitting me. Harder than that once-man or whatever did. How is this possible?"

"Free will Trans." And as Ronoh spoke his eyes shined into mine. "You see. You allowed me to train you. You prayed for strength and God answered your prayer by allowing me to bring you to the highest level I could. But against these creatures of flesh and darkness…"

"Alright, alright." I cut him off, "I'm tired of training and having the death of people on my hands. I am ready."

"Good." Replied Ronoh, "So now it begins. The fall of Illiathat. Be ready Trans. For the call to battle could come at any time, anywhere. Be ready to travel too. If you are needed someplace far away you will be given ample warning to get there in time, but I will not know the time of each battle beforehand. There may be more than one demon as well, so be ready for a hard fight." With that Ronoh turned to go.

"Oh and one more thing." He said as he walked away. "When you are called someplace. Feel free to get there anyway you want. As you travel and fight you will be hidden from the eyes of everyone save the enemy. Good luck Trans." And with that final comment Ronoh disappeared from sight.

The urges came on slowly at first; once every couple of weeks for a while. Sometimes they occurred after school, sometimes during, and sometimes before. Some even came in the middle of the night. Every time the urge hit I reacted instantly. I would fly forth from my bed, my desk, or wherever, and get to the next place of battle. I fought many battles over this time period. And I won each time. Most fights in the beginning consisted of easy one on one matches. I took on many different kinds of demons. Some were powerful, beast-like behemoths as easily as large as horses. Others looked like giant spiders, quick and agile. All were killed and all melted into the earth in the same thick, black ooze.

The battles were easy at first, but that soon changed. Quickly these creatures I was chosen to hunt and destroy began to group together. They traveled in twos most of the time and sometimes even in threes. I knew Illiathat was trying to find me now, and sending out more demons in an attempt to outmatch or catch me.

Ronoh found me after each fight. He always met me with words of encouragement, advice for future fights, or criticism about the past battle. This went on for months. I got into trouble with school for ditching out of class. They let me off after some pathetic explaining on my part. I mean I did get perfect marks on every test. My parents wanted me to go to some form of counseling to deal with all the "issues" they saw me as having. If only they could know the truth. But that would probably make them more upset, worried, or just further their idea that I into drugs. So I just went on with life. But as everything in my life had changed before, this phase was bound to change as well. I just never thought it would take the path it did. And even with my great strength and healing ability I have never fully recovered from the pain of that coming change.

Failure

I was in class. My teachers had, in a way, got used to the fact that sometimes I would just get up and run out of class. A classmate yelling, "Freak," or something of that nature usually chased after me and today was really no different. The urge hit me once again near the end of the day. I was in my final period before school got out, but the feeling told me I needed to go now, so I did. I jumped from my chair, leaving my books and my bag where they lay, and flew out of the classroom. Someone said something as I left, but my mind was focused on the feeling and I didn't really hear what was yelled after me. I took off out of the school and seconds after leaving the building, felt the now familiar feeling of invisibility come over me. It was not that I became transparent or anything similar to that. The feeling was more of an understanding. From that point onward I just knew that other people could no longer see me. By now, I had grown accustomed to this understanding.

I began sprinting off to the backside of school; facing in the direction the feeling seemed to pull me. As I gained speed and strength I began to jump. Soon I was bounding over the tops of the houses, with each jump taking me higher and on landing, gaining me more energy and power. I had gotten in the habit of praying and quieting my mind on the way to a fight and this time was no different. I asked the Lord for His strength and His blessing as I prepared for the coming battle. As I neared the place I was called to go I realized in mid-jump that I was being called to go to the very forest area I had been using to train with Ronoh. As I neared the final jump that would take me to the middle of the forest, I exploded off the ground with all my power and force, propelling my body skyward. I decided to gain some extra energy before this fight and knew that jumping high and landing hard might give me an edge. As I reached the pinnacle of my bound I looked down to see the tiny houses and cars below me. It almost looked like I was looking down out of an airplane and with that thought I began to plummet toward the ground.

I began gaining more and more speed. I turned my body and straightened myself to fly head first, straight down to gain terminal velocity for myself. I felt the wind whip through my hair and by my face as I neared the ground. When I was around twenty feet away from impact I flipped around in the air and exploded into the ground. I felt the energy of God flow forth into my body as I crushed the earth and stood to face the coming onslaught.

There in the clearing was a young child walking with the help of his mother. My resolve hardened as I saw the youth and joy contained in that little being. These two would not be taken. I felt the creatures before I saw them. There were three. This battle would be hard. I felt my invisibility disappear for a moment and I quickly approached the woman and her child. She seemed quite distressed at my sudden appearance and moved to put herself in front of her child as I walked toward them. I knew I had to get them out of there quick or while I was fighting one demon would be enough to drag both of the people into their realm.

"Excuse me, Ma'am." I spoke confidently, "Could I ask you to leave this area please. You see I am performing a science experiment with a rocket I designed and I would not want it to fall anywhere near you or your child."

Yeah, I know it was a pathetic excuse, but it was all I could come up with and the demons seemed to be getting restless with their target in sight. The lady consented easily enough, probably due more to the fact that I creeped her out than my fake rocket story. So she gathered her child up in her arms, turned and left.

I saw the hate burn and alight in the eyes and the minds of the three demons around me. They were still semi-concealed in shadows and foliage, so I had yet to get a good look at them. I could sense their rage at losing such an easy target, but I could also tell that they wanted revenge on the boy who had foiled them. As soon as the woman and her child were out of earshot I spoke.

"Well? What are you waiting for? Come on then, I'm ready."

The demons were obviously holding back. Probably due to the fact that they have had no idea I could see them. Then suddenly it happened. All at once from three different directions came a single attack. Three demons exploded from their hiding spots and came straight at me. Before they reached me I saw each one and mentally prepared for what it would take to defeat each of them.

One looked like a giant snake. It was easily twelve feet long and about as thick as a basketball for the most part of it. Its head looked like that of a snake. It had an elongated nose where huge fangs hung out on either side of its mouth, each at least two feet in length. This creature came fast writhing like a snake would, its top half coiled to strike. In addition, it also had arms coming out of the area that could be considered its torso. Both arms were huge and muscular and both looked extremely menacing.

The next demon looked more like a yeti than anything else. It was absolutely massive. It was easily ten feet tall and covered with black, bristly hair. It was as wide as a truck and moved with incredible speed and coordination for a beast of that size. Its arms and legs were enormous in bulk. The muscles could be seen bulging out from the body of this towering menace. It came forth with a terrifying roar; its arms raised and prepared to strike.

The final demon though, worried me the most. It moved faster than the other two and was clearly going to reach me first. As I looked at this creature I knew I had never fought anything like it before. It was the size of a full-grown silverback gorilla but much more massive. From the back of its elbows, two, three-foot spikes emerged and appeared to be razor sharp. The creature's fingernails also extended around three inches and looked like little daggers and were probably just as potent. This beast also had two spikes shaped like horns projecting out from his temples on each side of his head. Its back had a sheet of nail-like spikes jutting forth. I knew from my first look that this demon was formidable and extremely dangerous. I thought all of these things in a matter of moments. Then the spiked demon reached me and the last battle I would ever fight before the end of it all, began.

The spiked demon arrived first and came in for the initial kill. He reached back and attempted to slash open my throat with one sweep of his dagger-like talons. I stepped in quickly and caught his wrist in mid-swing. In that same instant the demon lowered his head and hoped that his continuing momentum would carry his horns through my face. I barely dropped to the ground quick enough to avoid the horns as they narrowly missed my head. I continued to the ground, planted one foot in the chest of this creature, rolled and kicked his body at the approaching snake. I saw the snake-like one try to evade the speeding body and spikes of the thrown demon, and he dodged semi-successfully, only catching a few puncture wounds from the nails that jutted out of the falling demon's back. I only got the opportunity to watch that occur for a split second before the yeti threw down both his fists, trying to crush me into the ground. But, I felt the yeti move in the air before he had even began his attack and I was ready. With terrifying speed I pulled me legs into my chest and shot them upward to meet the coming force of the assault. As my feet collided with the massive arms of the towering beast, I felt more energy come into me and I felt my advantage begin to come into play. The collision with my kick rocked the yeti back a step and just as quickly I was on my feet again.

The snake demon had already recovered from his painful collision with the spikes of the other one as the yeti rocked back, the snake struck out at my body from the side just as I arose. I stepped quickly back, as the acid filled fangs of the snake demon flew by the space that was just a second earlier occupied by my torso. As the snake extended past me, unable to stop its forward motion, I brought up my right arm and dropped an elbow across the spine of the snake-beast in front of me, punishing the monster down into the earth. Immediately I sensed movement in the air in front of me and began a quick back handspring to get out of the way. I never saw the right hook that was thrown by the recovered yeti, but I was glad that it didn't land because in a fight like this I knew I had no room for errors. Even taking one punch might put me off balance enough that the others could capitalize and finish the job.

As I flipped backward my mind seemed to slow down time so I could take in what was occurring during the revolutions. The spiked beast had collided with the snake and then continued with the force of my throw till it hit some rocks. It had recovered quickly enough and with a roar, was on its way back to join the battle. As I was flipping the yeti had stepped on the dropped snake-like beast and was pressing forward aggressively. I sensed the beast coming closer as I sprang back again onto my hands, halfway through a revolution. But, instead of letting my body continue the full cycle, I pressed off the ground with my arms and launched myself in the opposite direction, straight at the yeti's head. The quickness I had, combined with the move itself obviously confused the lumbering beast and set him off his guard. I landed a devastating kick to the face of this towering creature, sending him head over feet backward into the ground. I landed skillfully and prepared to finish off the yeti as it tried to stagger to its feet. Before I could move though I sensed the spiked demon attacking and quickly jumped off the ground around eight feet into the air. Right behind me a spiked elbow was thrust forward obviously in an attempt to skew my chest. I turned in the air and attempted to land another kick into the face of the spiked demon, but he brought up his other arm and I saw that my attack would be deflected. So to buy more time, instead of kicking out, I put my foot on his block and jumped back off of it, propelling myself to a safer distance. As I flew back I felt the air change around me again, but being in the air I had no way to change my direction or my speed. I felt the tail end of the snake wrap around my legs and it slammed me forcefully down into the earth. I was whipped painfully into some rocks that lay about and was almost stunned by the blows. I felt the tail unwrap from my legs and barely had time to roll over before the snake-like demon struck out.

I reached up just in time to grab hold of the two fangs that dripped acid around my head. Moments later the demon began to pummel my stomach with his two massive arms. I felt both pain and energy coarse into my mind and my body. But the creature's attack would be its downfall. I sensed the other two demons coming quickly to the scene of the struggle, so I acted swiftly. With the newfound strength given to me by the creature's blows, I ripped out the fang I held with my right hand and as the beast above me screamed out in pain and terror, I thrust the acid filled spike upward through the head of the demon. It writhed in agony and pain as I struggled out from underneath it. As soon as I was free it began to turn into slime and melt into the earth.

I stood now facing my opponents. Both had stopped suddenly and began to encircle me. A slight smile, if one could call it that began to spread on the spiked demon's deformed face. The yeti didn't seem to be smart enough to do anything but hate and kill. As the demons circled me I quieted my mind and a smile of my own slid across my face. But as soon as that smile crept onto my face, my now quieted mind registered something new. I felt something else. It was faint, but still there. I struck out with my mind, searching for the energy I felt. There, in the bushes. It was extremely faint but I soon saw why. A small, fat, bat-like creature was sitting on a branch peering out at the fight. And as the creatures circling me roared and attacked I knew why the spiked one had smiled. I have been seen and that fat, little spy demon was going to tell Illiathat all about me. As I dodged the attack from the two enraged demons, I watched the small spy fly off and return to its master. With mounting frustration I turned my attention back to the attacking demons.

With a yell of anger at having let down my guard, at having failed to notice the spy, and at having been recognized, I raised my power level to the highest height I had ever pushed it. With this newfound strength I struck out at the attacking demons. With two blocks I stopped both of the arms of the spiked one and planted a brutal forward kick into its chest, sending it flying back into a tangle of bushes and trees. I sensed the coming blow of the yeti and turned to meet the strike. As the yeti thrust forth his mighty arm in a gigantic swing, I made a swing of my own. Our fists met in an enormous collision. I felt my smaller hand shatter and crush the powerful bones

78

in the giant hand of my enemy. As the yeti reeled back in pain and roared with frustration, I jumped and landed quickly on the opposite side of the beast. Before the demon had time to turn and face me I lifted him up and tossed him horizontally skyward. I saw the spiked demon get up and charge me in the meantime, but at the same moment I knew I had just enough time to end the yeti before the spiked one reached me. As the yeti fell horizontally back to the earth, face looking skyward, I struck upward with both fists straight into the spine of the monster. As the demon's spine and my fists collided I felt the bones and ligaments that made up the beast's backbone shatter and tear as the strength of God poured forth into my arms. The yeti fell from my fists bent in half and began to dissolve into the dirt.

I wiped the sweat from my forehead and stared at my final opponent. There was pure hate reflected in the eyes of the monstrosity before me as I walked slowly toward it. The demon let out a vicious roar of pure anger and then, it began to change. First the horns on the demon's head elongated and sharpened. The dagger-like claws extended and thickened into a shape similar to short swords. The spines on the creature's back shot out forming a formidable wall of spikes and the already thick and powerful body grew even bigger. The demon seemed to grow into the body of the yeti. It let out a savage roar as its body expanded and grew taller. On the backside, under the sheet of spikes, a powerful tail grew. It was rough and scaled like that of the snake demon. And as the new demon stood fully formed and formidable, hate was not the only thing I saw reflected in this powerful creature's eyes anymore, confidence was now there as well. It looked at me with those hate filled eyes, and then, it attacked.

With a powerful charge the creature flung its hands toward me and several of the sword-like fingernails shot out and flew straight at me. With several quick moves I managed to sidestep and dodge the attack, but it left me off guard and as the last of the spikes flew past the massive demon was already upon me. With a speed I could never have anticipated the giant demon was nearly on top of me, horns lowered and heading straight for my chest. I grabbed both of the horns of the demon and held them a few inches away from my chest. The strain was nearly unbearable as I fought to hold the beast off. Then in one quick move the demon pulled his head back and kicked forward with one giant leg. The contact sent me flying away in the opposite direction. I collided with a tree and shattered right through the strong trunk. As my body skidded to a stop in the bushes the beast came lumbering on. I regained my breath and my senses moments before the creature was on top of me. I watched as the creature swiped one sword filled hand downward toward my prostrated body. I kicked my legs up over my head and rolled back just in time to dodge the swords. They scraped the dirt making several troughs right in the place where my body had been. Instantly I was on my feet with fire in my eyes. I would end this now. As I felt my strength increase the demon shot forth his other arm trying to stab through me with the spikes equipped there. I wasn't fast enough to get out of the way and as I turned my body to the side, several of the razor sharp spikes raked across my chest. As they contacted with my flesh I felt an unimaginable amount of pain race toward my brain. I jumped back and looked down onto my torn shirt, searching for blood and pieces of my flesh. The beast looked on with a cocky smile and cocked his head. I ripped off my shirt and looked again at my chest. All that appeared were several red lines where the swords had sliced. My skin had not been pierced. Then I felt it. Radiating outward from the slash marks massive amounts of pure energy flowed and continued to flow into my body. As I felt the energy of God reach new heights in my mind I looked back into the face of my adversary and now, it was my turn to smile again.

The creature stepped back in disbelief. A mingling of hate, confusion, and fear now mixed in the eyes I faced before me. I started to walk slowly toward the demon. One powerful arm was flung out from the demon as I approached. Several spikes exploded right for me. My confident smile never left my face and with a speed almost blurring reality I dodged and struck the projectiles out of my way and continued my gait toward the beast. The once-man bellowed out a howl of frustration and turned quickly to put his back in the direction facing me. The bed of spikes, that blanketed this beast's backside, quivered and suddenly exploded outward. I summoned the massive amounts of energy inside me and felt the power of God take over. With a speed that appeared impossible and seemed to border on instantaneous transportation I was immediately in front of the creature and away from the barrage of spikes. The eyes of the beast roared wide with fear at my sudden appearance before him. With a devastating forward blow I struck forth with a quick and potent kick to the giant demon's chest. I felt the familiar crunch of bones as my foot collapsed the ribcage of the demon before me. The beast stumbled back with a heaving chest, desperately attempting to draw another breath into its punctured and devastated lungs. The hideous thing before me struck out weakly as it sank down to its knees and fell onto its spike covered back. I walked forward and stood over the head of the once powerful monster. As the yellow eyes of the beast smoldered with hate and knowledge of its impending death I brought my foot up and slammed it powerfully down into the face of the beast, forever silencing the eyes of the terror before me. As the brute melted away I looked down at my tattered clothes and wounded body. Immediately Ronoh was before me and I will never forget the eyes of my mentor at that moment as he looked down into mine.

His face and his eyes were full of pain, sadness, and hurt. Nothing was physically wrong with this angel of God. The pain and sorrow I was witnessing was a reflection of Ronoh's soul and with that sight all time froze. In that one second I knew what had occurred and with one massive bound, consuming all the energy within, I was airborne.

Ronoh stood and watched as Trans sped off toward his home, even though he already knew what had occurred there. The demon spy had quickly returned to Illiathat to tell him what he had seen. Illiathat had immediately sent his most powerful warriors to the home of Trans and brutally murdered his family. Ronoh knew all this already because he had to stand and watch it happen.

"Sir?" Asked a powerful angel from behind the mourning captain, "Couldn't we have helped? Couldn't we have at least tried to protect his family?"

"No." Was Ronoh's only reply, "This is not our time yet. Trans must handle this alone."

Then Ronoh and his companion were gone and the forest was again left in silence.

I landed and the sight before me is forever burned and etched into the back of my mind. I burst through my front door, shattering the door from the frame. I nearly slipped as I flew into my house. I looked down and the floor was covered in a mess of blood. I ran around my home, the place of my birth and my raising. The place where I was grounded for the trouble I had got in. A place where I learned what love was from my parents and my sister. The place I found refuge from school and hope for the future was left a torn and bloody devastation. As I finished my search of my home I knew what had happened. I knew that the spy that had seen me had told Illiathat who I was and I knew he had taken my family himself. I sank to my knees as the pain and the tears overtook me. My mind burned and blurred as the sting of tears flowed down over me eyes and my face. I saw before me the faces of my family. I saw the terror and pain they experienced as the demons appeared and began the slaughter. Ronoh appeared and laid his hands on me, but even his consolation would not help, and through sobs and tears I cried out to God for mercy. I prayed for anything to take the pain away. I prayed for my family to be back unhurt. And as I let the words and pain fall from my lips to a listening God, deep down I knew that my wishes were not going to come true. I remembered the words of Ronoh, his warning. I saw how Illiathat meant to weaken me here. And as the last of my tears fell after unknown hours had passed, before me I felt an unbelievable hate and anger burn and begin to consume my soul. Illiathat will die. With that thought consuming all rational in my mind I stood powerfully and purposefully and prepared to go on the hunt for this murderer. As I began to storm out of my front door and leave the blood and destruction behind, Ronoh suddenly appeared to block my path.

"Where do you think you're going?" Ronoh said with power behind his voice.

"I'm going to kill Illiathat. This will end now."

"That is his plan." Countered my friend, "He did this to bring you out. He knows he can defeat you and he has hoped you would walk into your own death. I know you are in pain, but do not forsake the earth because of this attack."

As I looked into the eyes of the archangel of God standing before me I smiled with tear stained eyes.

"I know his plan." I said, "I know he wants me to face him now, out of anger and with feelings of revenge. This is why I will do just what he wants."

And with a cunning smile I wiped the tears from my eyes and walked out of my house with my mentor in tow.

The Beginning of the End

I walked in silence with my angelic companion till I reached the place of my training and my last battle. It was there that I finally broke the silence.

"I have decided to end this." I began. "Illiathat must be destroyed and this game of delaying him is not a means to the end."

My giant friend just looked into my eyes. "What do you propose?"

"I want to call him out, and not just him, but all his minions as well."

"You don't have the power or the strength to beat him and he is expecting you to try and fight him now. If you do so you will lose."

I just shook my head. "You're right." I consented. "But I am not going to be the one to destroy them."

"OK, you got my attention."

And with that Ronoh and I began to talk. I explained my plan of attack. We discussed the weaknesses and strengths that arose. Ronoh continued to try and convince me a full frontal attack would fail. I tried to assure him it wouldn't.

"I feel the conviction of God that the final battle is upon me." I said. "I know I am not ready. I know that if I attempted this fight with my own God-given abilities I would fail. But that is what I am not going to do. And I am going to fight him whether you agree with me or not."

My powerful friend looked into the hardened resolve burning within my eyes and finally consented.

"If you feel that the time for the end has arrived, than I stand behind you fully. But I pray you are not making this decision on anger. That is what Illiathat expects."

"I know. But what I have in store, he could never imagine. Tomorrow at first light I am going to the Valley of Shadows."

With that last remark I looked into the face of my friend. "Thank you Ronoh. You have been a great friend and counselor. Your presence and your help have blessed my life. I will miss you. Good bye."

And with those final parting words I turned and walked back to my lonely home. When I arrived I found no visible evidence of the remains of my family. Even the blood that was splattered about had gone. I slept that night in my parent's bed. As I lay down to sleep I felt the presence of God enter my room and comfort my mind. And with a parting prayer and thoughts of Heaven I drifted peacefully into the waiting embrace of sleep. Tomorrow it would all be over I told myself, one way or another.

The Strength of the Lord

As the sun lifted its head and began to smile on the earth I arose from my parent's bed and slipped into the shower. Right from the start of the day I already felt my power level increasing and I knew God was with me. I ate little for the need for food escaped me that morning and I dressed in comfortable clothes. I wore a loose pair of jeans and a comfortable t-shirt. I laced my shoes on tight knowing today would be a day I could never be fully prepared for. I left my house and started to run. I didn't even bother to jump as I raced toward the place where Illiathat and his army disappeared from the earth. I felt the strength of the Lord increase quickly today and after a few miles I was nearly flying toward the battlefield. My feet nimbly touched the ground before exploding my body onward as I tore to my destination. Mountains, water, and oceans passed by in a blur, till finally I arrived.

The Valley of Shadows was a desert. I noticed that no vegetation grew in or around the area as I surveyed it. It was a massive valley rimmed on all sides by imposing cliffs that towered easily a hundred feet on either side. The valley floor and surrounding area was composed of mainly dirt and rock. It all took on an imposing air as I jumped down onto the valley floor from the rim. Once there I glanced at my environment. The valley floor, mostly stone, was not flat at all like I expected. Chunks of rock and stone jutted out of the earth at

88

sporadic places, almost giving the area a labyrinth-like appearance. All seemed quiet and empty, and then I felt the power.

It hit me like a blow across the chest. The evil that this place contained was immense and terrifying. I had to close my eyes and quiet my mind under the screams of the trapped and imprisoned demons. As my mind and body relaxed I felt that slight nudge pushing me to continue. I jumped back up to the valley rim and gazed out over the scene. I took one knee, bowed my head, and threw up a last prayer for guidance and protection. Then it all began.

"Illiathat!" I announced with authority. "The time has come for us to meet."

I waited in silence as my voice echoed across the valley and bounced against its walls.

"Show yourself you coward. No more hiding or sending your pawns to do your dirty work. This time we finish this forever."

Again, only the echo of my voice and a consuming deathly silence greeted me. There was no reply to my call.

"By the power of God and the strength of the Lamb I command you and all foul creatures that follow you to show yourselves!"

"You command me?" The voice of this lord of demons pierced my soul and a cold shiver entered my bones. "Do you really wish to die so soon? We could have had a lot more fun you know. Your family was delightful to meet."

I roared out in anger, "Show yourself!"

"In due time my friend. Are you so eager to join them?"

"I will destroy you. You are a coward and murderer!"

"Oh will you?" And with those piercing words a man seemed to walk out of thin air down before me on the valley floor. He was dressed casually in what appeared as old world garb. He wore a loose fitting white shirt, unbuttoned half way down and blowing in the wind. He also wore strong leather pants, masterfully sewn, with a huge S-shaped sword strapped to a strong leather belt around his waist.

"You? A lone boy with no army behind him?" mockingly called out the demon lord.

"No army. Just you and me, alone. The king of demons versus a boy."

"Don't poor mouth with me, you foolish child. I know who you are and what you are capable of. I am not afraid. Come then, if you are so eager to die. Let's get this over with. Oh and by the way. I do so much appreciate being loosed into this pitiful world once again. I must remember to thank you sometime for calling me out of that wretched darkness."

As the lord of demons finished those last taunting words I bounded off the rim of the valley and landed with a small explosion nearly twenty feet away from this enemy.

"Stupid child. You have come to your death." With that remark I felt an ominous sensation and before my eyes and my senses all of the remaining army of Deteath materialized around me. I watched and felt as thousands of demon once-men arrived, all hideous in strength, size, and appearance. They surrounded me and seemed to be foaming with hate and an uncontrollable desire to see my heart ripped from my chest. Illiathat appeared to be the only one holding them back.

"You coward!" I spat at the demon lord. "You boast of your power yet you bring in your whole army to kill one small child. You are pathetic."

"You misunderstand me Boy. If I commanded it, you would already be dead. It was not I who commanded, in the name of that Deity you so worship, to bring them here. You, Trans, brought my whole army out to watch, and watch they will, as I slowly rip the life from your frail body."

With that, a roar of approval burst out from the massing troops surrounding me.

"Well come on then!" I yelled. "You killed my family and countless others. But the terror you have caused stops now! You are nothing to me and into nothing you will go!"

Illiathat smiled and calmly, wickedly, confidently, he replied, "You are already dead."

With those final hate filled words Illiathat, the Prince of demons and lord of the House of Deteath walked slowly forward to meet me. As he approached he drew forth the menacing S-shaped sword from his waist. One side was serrated and he held it in front of him with both hands; that same cocky smile pulled across his face. I felt waves of pure evil and power resonating outward from the being that faced me. I stepped back and dropped into a crouch. Then before I had time to even think another thought, Illiathat was attacking. I barely had time to dodge as the demon king ripped the air with his blade in a cutting slash. I stepped back and felt the razor sharp edge of the blade slice through my t-shirt, a hairs width from my skin. Before I could even resume drawing breath the sword was again arched and swung downward at my head. I leapt quickly to one side as the blade again, cut through my shirt, this time ripping it clean off. Instantly I placed both of my hands on those of the demon lord, holding them down. I was trying to pin his sword against the earth. I felt a chilling and penetrating cold enter my body from my hands as I held his arms and his sword down.

"You are too slow Boy." Spat Illiathat, "You should know when you are outmatched."

"You're wrong." I replied as the king demon threw off my hands and resumed his attack. Yet, it was at that point that I knew I was in trouble. I was holding down the arms of this demon with all my God-given strength and he threw off my grip as if I was barely touching him. I was forced back as the demon brought up his sword and began another slash at my midsection. I flipped back to one side onto my right hand, planted it in the earth, and met the sword handle of Illiathat with a powerful kick. On contact I felt some of the true power I had only sensed moments before. My foot was almost broken as I contacted the swing of that sword with my kick. I flipped backward back up to my feet as the sword of Illiathat bounced back. He came at me again, this time thrusting forward his cruel weapon. I jumped and felt the sword slide inches under my body as I elevated. I kicked out in an attempt to land a blow on the face of this seemingly unstoppable enemy. Instantly an arm of the demon was up and with evident ease

Illiathat caught my foot and flung me over his shoulder into the earth. I slid several feet before I eventually stopped, digging up dirt and rock as my body smashed forward.

"You see foolish child," said Illiathat as he walked over to where I stood, "you have no chance against me. I knew you would come here to avenge your parents. I knew that through your stupidity and pride you would release not only me, but my minions as well. You are predictable and now you are dead." With that remark the powerful demon lifted his menacing sword over his head. I looked up from the ground into the eyes of the beast before me and smiled.

"Why are you smiling you fool? Your death is upon you," snarled Illiathat.

"No. I come in the name of the almighty God and the Lamb. Your death is upon you."

Illiathat roared with anger and cut downward with all his terrifying power. I brought forth the power Illiathat had given to me. As the deadly sword of the king of demons ripped through the air straight for me I watched, as the terrifyingly fast swing seemed to slow down. My mind sped up and everything around me seemed to move in slow motion. I gathered the strength inside of me and struck out from my now sitting position with an unbelievable right hook. I met the side of the sword with a quick and powerful blow as it careened downward and watched as the demon blade shattered against the power and the might of God.

Illiathat nearly fell back under the force of the collision. His face registering a look of shock and anger as his sword broke and exploded out in a shower of razor sharp fragments. I was back on my feet before the demon lord has regained his composure. I kicked out at the beast's chest. Illiathat was not caught of guard and he raised his arms in defense and blocked the attack. But the power behind the kick sent him skidding backward under its pressure. I pressed my attack and moved with the amazing quickness Ronoh had taught me how to use. Before the demon had stopped his skid backward I was already behind him and before he could register what was happening I struck out with a gigantic forward punch and connected with the back of the monster. Illiathat was rocked forward and landed hard on his face as his body continued to propel onward several more feet. As he quickly rolled over onto his back, I was already landing from a jump, straight onto the creature's torso, driving me knee deep into the chest of this fiend.

"This is over!" I yelled into the face of my adversary as I drew back my fist to drive it forward into the head of Illiathat. I was met with laughter from my pinned enemy.

"Far from it mortal. This is only the beginning."

I drove my arm forward toward the face of Illiathat with the determination to crush the skull of the thing underneath me. But, as my fist neared its destination something stopped my blow. I felt my fist slam into something in the air before me and that invisible wall stopped my attack dead in its tracks. Again Illiathat only laughed. I pulled my arm back to try again and as my arm cocked and I prepared to strike out again, the demon underneath me roared out. I felt a massive amount of energy pulsate into the world from the monster and as I tried to punch down again I felt the true strength of the foe I sought to vanquish. I was flung backward off the demon by some unseen and terrifyingly awesome power. I felt my body being lifted up and flung back with tremendous force. I continued to fly back faster and faster. I saw the demon hordes jump and scatter, some too slowly and my body rocked into them, as my being shot away from Illiathat. I felt the energy around me build and gather. Suddenly I collided with a cliff face surrounding the valley. My body smashed against rock and I was forced back into it with a powerful evil I had never felt before. Pieces of stone shattered and flew outward as my body was pummeled into the cliff face. I fell to me knees after the massive blow, desperately trying to regain the breath that had been knocked from my body. I felt blood begin to flow freely from my nose and the pain that flowed in with the energy from that blow attacked my mind and body with a fury I had never before felt throughout all my days of training and battle. Illiathat merely stood and laughed.

"You stupid boy. Did you think you had a chance? I was only toying with you. You have no idea of the power that I have contained within this vessel. You have only tasted the tip of the things I am capable of. And before you die and draw your final breath under my feet, you shall know the terror that I am."

With an inhuman howl Illiathat looked skyward and something began to change. I felt the evil power of the demon before me flow outward. The force of it pressed me back against the face of the cliff I had just collided with and before my wide and terrified eyes Illiathat transformed.

I watched in horror as the skin and body of the powerful demon lord before me ripped back and fell away. What emerged was something I could have never imagined and something I would never forget. A slithering, black, and gnarled entity came forth from the skin of the King of Deteath. The thing that immerged vaguely resembled a human at first sight, but soon it began to change further. The creature grew in size dramatically and finally stopped at an imposing fifty-feet. It was a massive thing, all muscle, and resounding with power. It was covered with a black and leathery skin that pulsated with energy. Its head was ringed with a threatening crown of protruding spikes, each appearing to be at least five feet in length and razor sharp. Illiathat's two arms that now hung menacingly at his sides were rippling with muscle. His legs had the same frightening strength, as did his whole being. As the body of this now immense beast took full form, two enormous wings flew into the world from the back of the beast, extending out to their full length and filling the valley in which the demon stood. After that the beast let out a deafening roar to the apparent joy of his surrounding minions that bounced and echoed off the encircling cliffs. The noise was so menacing and horrible it almost forced me to cover my ears to block out the appalling sound. Finally as the body of Illiathat finished its transformation, the giant bat-like wings enfolded over the shoulders of the beast forming a cloak over its back and shoulders.

"Now you can see the true power of the might you are foolish enough to challenge. This world belongs to me now and there is nothing that can stop me. This world's faith is dead. Where is your God now?"

I looked into the face of this towering creature.

"He is right where he has always been." I replied, breathing heavily and trying to stand up straight. "He is here within me."

Illiathat just laughed producing a horrible and cruel noise.

"This is over." He said with a grin. "I have had enough of you. Kill him."

And with that last command I watched as the thousands of demons scattered amongst the valley howled with delight and began to race toward me. In sight of such massive numbers and overwhelming odds, all I could do was call out to God. I began to pray for help and deliverance. Suddenly a mighty sound struck forth and silenced the oncoming horde. It was the sound of a trumpet, but far greater. It filled the valley with an awesome noise and stopped many of the demons in their onslaught. The sound seemed to carry on indefinitely and then it stopped just as suddenly as it began. I looked out over the Valley of Shadows and began to rub my eyes. For tiny sparkles of light began to appear in the sky. They seemed to come from everywhere and nowhere and at the same time appeared to be growing in size. Then it happened. The demons wailed out in a scream of confusion and frustration and instantly began to charge anew. Suddenly a line of angels seemed to lift out of the ground across the valley floor in front of me. All of them caught up in the glory and the power of the living God. They shined forth brilliantly, wings extended, massive swords raised for battle. They called out in unison as the waves of demons approached.

"For the glory of God and the Lamb!"

Their voices shook the valley and suddenly more appeared swooping down to meet the coming rush. Hundreds and hundreds of angels flew in from every direction to join the impending battle. The light was almost too much. Then I saw Ronoh standing in the front line, sword drawn. He looked back for a moment and our eyes met. I heard him speak into my mind.

"We cannot hold them forever my friend. Now is your time. Illiathat must be destroyed. Go and may the grace of the Lord shine forth and protect you."

I picked myself off the ground and watched as the lines of frenzied demons met and exploded against the defending angels of God. For a moment I thought the angels would actually overcome the threat, but then I looked closer. The warriors of God fought with amazing strength and skill, but the demons were slowly overrunning them. I watched as several lights flickered and then fell, followed by others, as fallen men empowered by demons cut down the defending angels.

"Ronoh was right. They can't win." I thought.

I saw Ronoh fall under the blows of a giant attacking demon. I screamed out in pain and frustration for my friend and mentor. I flooded my body with the energy of God that resided within and prepared to attack. Then I saw Ronoh reappear in another area of the fight, strengthening his brothers and leading the defense. I would not let the sacrifice of these angels go unanswered and with a mighty leap I burst skyward from the ground and flew straight for the towering Illiathat. I had no idea how to defeat an enemy of that size, but none of that mattered to me now. I felt the heat of battle and the strength of God embrace my mind and I was going to kill that beast no matter the cost.

Illiathat let out a howl of frustration at the sight of the new fighters. He crouched and prepared to jump into the heart of the battle. Then he saw me speeding through the air straight toward him. Our eyes met and for an instant I thought I saw victory. I turned my body and angled my trajectory, determined to drive my foot into the gigantic chest of the enormous monster. Suddenly a grotesque hand came speeding through the air and swatted me away. I felt the palm of the beast hit my entire body and I flew back into the wall of the cliff beside me. I felt unbelievable pain and energy simultaneously enter my body. I struggled to stand as the angels fought on relentlessly below me, their numbers dwindling quickly. With a roar of hope and anger I opened the contained energy within me and felt it flex out from me in a moment of mind shocking power. I felt my body being lifted off the ground with the energy contained within. I felt the might of God as I continued to yell and loose the power I had been gifted to wield. My body rose a few feet from the earth and without even pushing off against the cliff face I exploded toward the demon king before me. I felt waves of power flowing out from my body as I rocketed toward my enemy. As I neared the beast I sensed another swing from a giant arm that meant to drive me downward into the earth. Without thinking I summoned the power within me that was desperately trying to come out and changed directions. I was flying. The realization came without any shock or surprise. The colossal arm and hand of Illiathat swung downward and cleanly missed. Illiathat's face had barely enough time to register the shock of my newfound ability before I turned my body and drove my foot forward into the beast's giant face, right between the eyes. Illiathat rocked back under the force of the blow and again struck out. I nimbly dodged the second arm swing and prepared to attack again. Suddenly I felt the blow I sensed only moments too late. Illiathat's other arm had flashed out and sent me sailing across the valley and again into a wall of the surrounding cliff. Before I even had time to collide with the wall of the surrounding rock Illiathat had charged toward me and at the same instant I slammed into the face of the cliff, the transformed demon lord drove a mighty fist into the rock where I had landed. The beast drove his fist forward smashing me deep into the mountain of stone and dirt. I barely had enough time to raise my power before the fist crushed me into the wall. Illiathat pulled back his arm and I fell limply out of the rock face. My near exhausted body plummeted to the earth from half way up the hundred-foot face. As I fell I glanced at the remaining Host of Heaven. Their battle was fierce and although the angels' numbers had been cut down drastically; they still fought on with an unimaginable strength and determination. Then my body slammed into the hard, rocky earth. I looked up just as in time to see Illiathat raise one immense leg and I flinched as he slammed it down into me and into the earth. I felt a terrifying pressure and then everything went dark.

Final Moments

As darkness closed over my mind I felt the pain that had been stabbing continually into it since the beginning moments of battle fade and drift away. I was alone in my mind and in the darkness consuming it, waiting for death. But death would not come to me then, and in that moment that contained all moments I saw for the first time the entire picture of who and what I was. Something clicked again. I finally recognized the truth. I saw how I gained enormous amounts of power on my way to the final battle without taking up energy to begin with. I recognized the truth behind my ability to absorb energy. The ability to transfer energy into my being was not my true talent. That was a side effect that came from my real gift. I thought back over the time I spent growing in the Lord and trying to understand myself. I remembered the lessons taught to me by Ronoh and I remembered what he had said. The words "free will" echoed in my mind. The power of God that flowed into me was not due to the things I made contact with. The power that I gained poured forth from the Creator himself and all I had to do to channel that power was ask. I let that life-altering truth settled down over my mind. In the darkness I finally understood and for the last time in my life, everything within me changed at once.

Illiathat stood overlooking the one-sided battle. A smile etched on his sick and gnarled face. He watched as his powerful minions began to overrun the few remaining struggling angels. His foot still pressing downward over the life he had thought he had snubbed out. But suddenly, that leg was thrown upward. Illiathat's massive form was thrown off balance and I flew into the air from the hole in the earth where a few seconds prior my dying body had lay. Illiathat got one quick glance at the power and enormous strength that now radiated from my elevated being before I shot out from my spot in the air right into the brute's chest, landing a blow that sent him flying over the battlefield. The fighting demons looked up in stunned silence as their great and mighty leader was thrown clear across the valley. My body remained hovering in mid-air fifty-feet above the valley floor, the pure and unlimited power of the Almighty God flowing outward in terrifying waves. My whole person seemed to glow with the power of God. Below the angels felt the strength and might of their Lord rise in them as it surged forth from me. They took up the cry of the Lord and resumed their fight with increased strength and power, cutting down and through, demon after demon. Illiathat hit the far wall with an explosion of rock and landed powerfully into the earth. The demon lord's eyes rose to meet mine, a faint hint of fear shown out of them. I began to move toward the beast. I felt the power of God embracing me in the air, as it poured into me from everywhere at once. Illiathat roared and charged across the valley to meet me. His speed was nearly unimaginable and he brought up a massive arm and flung it out to swat me from the sky. I raised my right hand to meet it and before it was even close to my body I sent the overwhelming power of God out from my hand into his attack. Illiathat's fist flew backward under the protection of God. He attacked again, this time with the other arm, striking out with enormous speed and power. Again the pure energy of the Lord that consumed my whole being shot forth at my command and flung the demon's arm harmlessly out of the way.

"It is over!" I announced.

And as Illiathat began his reply contained within an inhuman wail of anger and hatred, I thrust out both arms and sent forth a massive wave of energy that sent the demon king flying back into the cliffs behind him. His body shattered and rocked the whole basin as it rammed into the wall under the force of God. Before the King of Demons could regain his footing I sent all the power enclosed in my being out into his. I felt pure light explode from both my hands as I summoned the full force and might of the God I believed in. The light was unlike anything I have every experienced. It was so bright that it appeared to be burning as it shot from my arms. It hit Illiathat directly in the chest and pinned him back against the rocks. The giant demon raised one arm and tried to shield himself, as he fought and struggled against the beam of energy that continually hammered him into the cliff wall. All of it was to no avail. I felt massive amounts of energy leave my body, but as it flowed forth, more seemed to pour in from every direction. I felt the heat and strength of the light of God rise and burn with the ferocity of unlimited power and unfathomable strength. I saw Illiathat writhe and howl under the force contained within the merciless light and the evident pain it brought. A thick, black cloud of smoke began to issue forth from the burning body of the demon king. With the coming smoke, Illiathat's wail increased in pain as the pure might of Christ continued to stream out of me and into this creature of darkness. Slowly the light began to fully consume the whole being of the monster. Illiathat struggled and struck out against the light, but all his efforts could not free him from the constraints the power held over him. I watched as pieces of the terror before me began to be ripped away and fall disintegrating downward into the earth. With one final endeavor I sent all the power my vessel could contain into the now terrified beast. I pushed onward and under the strain of the invading light Illiathat exploded and the whole valley shook under the force of the blast. A thousand black pieces seemed to rise into the morning air and were consequently consumed by the light that still eagerly sought to devour them.

As the final pieces of Illiathat dissolved into nothingness I felt the energy that had enraptured me before fade and flow away, leaving me beyond the point of exhaustion. I had just enough time before I passed out to turn and see the remaining demons melting into the earth as I fell back to the ground. With a final feeling of peace, and a knowledge that all was finally done, I let darkness consume me once again and I fell contented to the earth below.

Underneath Trans the surviving warriors of Heaven glanced skyward as the limp body of their hero fell silently to the earth. The remaining pieces of the dissolving demons continued to sizzle and melt out of existence. Ronoh appeared directly below the falling vessel, catching him gently and setting him softly upon the earth. The surviving angels picked themselves up and began to tend to their wounded numbers while simultaneously watching the fatally wounded flicker out of existence. As Trans slept on Ronoh, in one massive and powerful hand, lifted his sword aloft in a glorifying gesture of victory. The angels that had followed him into battle also raised their weapons and their voices as another earth rocking cry broke forth.

"For God and for the Lamb!"

The final bits and pieces of the conquered demons sizzled into nothingness and the celebration began. The heavenly warriors blazed forth brilliantly with the power and light of God. Some sang out in praise. Others fell to their knees in prayer. All celebrated the victory over the enemy and in it all, gave God the glory He deserved.

Last Request

After what seemed an eternity of silence I felt the warm radiance of sunlight pressing against my closed eyelids. I blinked back against the warm glow and slowly sat up.

"Well it certainly is about time. I was beginning to wonder how long you could sleep." The sound of Ronoh's strong and gentle voice filled me with an awesome joy as it washed over my mind. As my eyes adjusted to the glare of the sun I looked around for my mentor. I found him sitting on a rock a few feet away, his massive form resting against the earth.

"Well done, Trans. To be honest I thought we were defeated when you went down that last time. But by the grace of God here we are!"

He said that last part with a laugh and a smile. His eyes danced with merriment that my own reciprocated. We had won after all. God had been faithful and had delivered his people. I fell back into the earth with a laugh and felt the sun wash over my body.

"What now?" I asked suddenly. "What happens to me? I feel as if my life is over."

"Well," Ronoh began, "actually it is, Lad. You gave it up with that final fight with Illiathat."

"What? What do you mean? You...you mean I'm dead?"

Ronoh looked at me and laughed. "Well not just yet friend. You're still here on earth aren't you?"

"Well I guess, but what do you mean?"

Ronoh continued, "Remember your decision to face Illiathat no matter the cost." I nodded, "Well as Illiathat crushed you into the earth you made the choice to channel God's energy through your body. All of the angels fighting felt it as you did. It was the choice that won the war. We would have lost had you not made that move. Sadly the holiness of God is too much for any human vessel to come into contact with. Even one as blessed as you. It has killed your body."

Before I could interrupt with more questions, Ronoh raised one hand and continued, "You see, God has recognized your sacrifice and is keeping you here until he is content that you have fully accomplished everything you have been destined to do."

"What else do I have to do? I can't believe there is more." I replied incredulously.

"Look within yourself, Lad. I know there is some desire buried within."

I felt my gaze drop as I reached back into my mind, searching for some lost aspiration. Finally I looked up.

"I would like to tell the world what has happened."

"They won't believe you, you know."

"I know, but I still want to. Will God grant me the time to write down my story?"

"Ask him yourself. But as for me I have to be going now. You know, people to see and all. Take care, Trans, I'm sure I'll be seeing you again some time soon."

"Thanks Ronoh. You have been a good friend and companion. I will never forget you."

With a smile we embraced, a scrawny young boy and a giant archangel and warrior of God. After, Ronoh stepped back and with a smile he transformed into the shining warrior of God I had seen before and flew off into the heavens.

"I'll miss you." I said as the shining fighter disappeared into the clouds above. I stayed for a while in the valley caught up in prayer and thankfulness, praising the God of deliverance and power. Soon after that, I walked off toward home.

When I arrived back at home I ate when I needed to and sleep when I got tired. The rest of the time I spent writing. I just put the pen to the paper and let my thoughts take me back to the first days of my life. The words just flowed from my hand as I let the thoughts and images tumble from my mind. After several days and many pages I had finished my story. I don't expect any of you out there who read this to naturally believe it. I know it seems to come from out of nowhere. I understand that most of you refuse to even acknowledge that a real God might exist. That's OK. As a very wise man once told me, even if you don't believe in God, that doesn't mean He is not out there. All I hope to do with this story is help just one person. If one person can be encouraged through this tale I will have accomplished what I set out to do. Now all is over for me. I'm not sure what is going to happen when my life is finally taken from me. I know I will go off to meet my Creator and I am both excited and terrified at the thought of it. But for now I guess I am done. I hope my story helps. Good-bye.

-Trans

After Thoughts

This last bit here is included for a few reasons. For one, I think some of you out there may be wondering how a true first-person narrative could contain the viewpoints of other people if the story is truly an autobiography. Well, as I finished my story and presented it to Ronoh, an interesting event occurred, interesting enough for me to include this last bit. As Ronoh held the finished work between his hands it started to glow. I stared in amazement as the papers began to thicken right before me eyes. Ronoh handed them back to me and told me that the work was now complete. He said it needed a little touch. As I flipped quickly through it I noticed that two more character's parts had been inserted into my story. I saw that the thoughts and actions of Illiathat and my friend Ronoh were now integrated into the whole story. Praise God was all I could think.

As I prepared to leave my life behind, I left several copies of my story behind. I knew sooner or later people would get curious as to where my family and I had disappeared to and come looking. I hoped my story would be found and read from there. So I left my house and traveled to the forest where I had trained since that first day. There I met Ronoh. He was waiting for me and he smiled as I walked into the field. We met in the middle, exchanged pleasant greetings and a warm embrace. After that he asked if I was ready. I told him of course not and with a laugh we both leapt off the ground and flew straight up into the heavens. The rest of the story is not my part to tell. You'll find out what it's like one day if you really want to. Till then.

Reality

The neon red of my alarm clock ticked to 3:00 A.M. as I stared into the soft glow of my computer monitor, the faint light that shown out illuminated most of my now dark room. I clicked the save button and sank back into my chair. I let my mind run over the images I had just created. I saw pictures of Trans and his fight against the demons. I saw once again the final blow that destroyed Illiathat. I saw the might of Ronoh as he fought bravely against the demon hordes, and I wished I could forever escape into that world I had just created. It seemed to be much happier than my own. It was one where the good guys actually won. I closed down my computer and shut it off.

"Oh well." I murmured as I climbed into bed, "Maybe today when I get up, school will be different."

My mind danced with the thoughts of the coming day. I wondered what names I would be called, and who on this day, would knock me down or make fun of me. And I wondered if it would ever stop. As I let my head sink into my bed I felt the familiar sting of tears as they rolled out of my eyes and slid down onto my pillow.

"If only I was bigger," I thought, "if only I was cooler, if only I was good at sports."

A thousand fears, doubts, and questions plagued my mind. I watched like a silent witness as the insecurities I had been fighting back broke out in the core of my being and assaulted my mind. I felt them bore deep into my soul, crushing my heart and my spirit. These inner demons brought out everything I felt was wrong with myself and made me feel the full weight of the failure I believed I was. I silently wept and cried out in prayer to God. I prayed for peace, for friends, for guidance. I prayed for enough strength to just get through tomorrow and I prayed I would not get made fun of anymore. As my mind raced with pain, sadness, and everything I believed wrong with myself I at last began to feel the pull of sleep beginning to take its hold. Finally exhaustion took over and I began to slip into slumber.

As the small boy silently wept, fighting his thoughts of insecurity and pain that were keeping the warm embrace of sleep just out of reach, he never noticed the massive figure that stood in the corner of his room. A gigantic man, who was easily seven feet tall and substantially built, slowly walked over to where the young boy lay and placed one massive hand on his small, shaking shoulder. Slowly the fears and the nightmares faded from the boy's mind. Peace entered his heart and somehow, he slept. And somewhere, deep inside, something told him tomorrow would be OK.

The angel standing over the boy looked down onto his small sleeping frame.

"You are destined for great things, Lad." He said silently. "Never give up hope."

That night the massive angel stayed, standing over the sleeping boy. One hand pressed against the shoulder of the child, protecting his mind from the daggers of the demons that tried to cut and hack at the boy's insecurities. Through it all, the boy slept on, unaware of the authority and strength that was standing right in his room and oblivious to the power and greatness that was dwelling right in his heart.

Troy Anston

About the Author

Alec Hanson is currently a 22 year old senior at the University of California, Berkeley. He does not describe himself as an author in any way. He has always enjoyed reading and somehow found himself writing a story one day that took hold of his mind and imagination and would not let him go until it was finished.

Printed in the United States
16297LVS00001B/228